THE BILLIONAIRE'S ACCIDENTAL BRIDE

A BILLIONAIRE ROMANCE By..

KIMMY LOVE

Fancy A FREE BWWM Romance Book??

Join the "**Romance Recommended**" Mailing list today and gain access to an exclusive **FREE** classic BWWM Romance book along with many others more to come. You will also be kept up to date on the best book deals in the future on the hottest new BWWM Romances.

* Get FREE Romance Books For Your Kindle & Other Cool giveaways

* Discover Exclusive Deals & Discounts Before Anyone Else!

* Be The FIRST To Know about Hot New Releases From Your Favorite Authors

Click The Link Below To Access This Now!

Oh Yes! Sign Me Up To Romance Recommended For FREE!

Already subscribed?

OK, Read On!

Summary

Annaya's wild streak has often got her into trouble before but this situation is something else.

After going to Vegas for a girl's weekend, one drink led to another and before she knew it she was waking up in bed next to a man she did not know.

As it turns out, that man was Billionaire playboy Jack Casali and this was not just a one night stand, they also got married too!

Annaya now has to face up to the reality of being known by the press as the "Billionaire's Accidental Bride" and the two strangers face a race against time to get their accidental marriage annulled and putting this incident behind them.

However, it seems that fate might have other plans for them...

Copyright Notice

Contents

Chapter 1

Lights. Glitz. Glamor It was all the norm for Jack Casali. He was the son of business tycoon, Brandon Casali, who'd made his fortune building casinos and making a name for himself as one of the wealthiest entrepreneurs in Vegas. Jack grew up among roulette wheels and showgirls and consequently, at thirty-one years of age, he'd become quite a reckless man with a taste for the high life.

That day was no different. Dressed in a tuxedo that cost as much as a small car, with his jet black hair styled like a 40's film star and a confident smile on his face that made women swoon, he stood at the entrance of one of his father's casinos and smiled even more widely when he saw an expensive Ferrari pull up and his best friend Lewis step out and throw his keys to the valet.

The two met five years earlier at a charity gala held at a hotel, where Jack had come to pick up upper-class women and Lewis had come to represent his father's pharmaceutical corporation. They'd clicked straight away as two young men of fortune and since spent many a night painting the town red and making the most of their youth and wealth.

Lewis rubbed his hands together with an expectant grin on his face and greeted Jack with a friendly slap on the back. "Good evening, Mr. Casali," he said teasingly. "Are you ready for another wild night?"

"Me? Wild? I'm here to represent the values of Casali Casinos."

Lewis laughed at that and shook his head with amusement. They both knew that they weren't the best representations of their fathers' tenacity and industrialism, but neither of them took it too much to heart. It was much easier just to enjoy the life they'd been given and try not to do anything that would affect their fathers' reputations too badly.

The two men made their way into the casino, ready for a night of champagne, gambling and beautiful women, and Jack wasn't disappointed. The second he stepped through the rotating door and placed his foot upon the deep red carpet, he spotted the most beautiful woman he had ever seen drinking a glass of champagne and laughing loudly, surrounded by a group of other women.

The woman who d caught his eye was dark-skinned

and had frothy light-brown hair, which spilled down her back. She had a dazzling smile that seemed to light up the whole casino and big, dark, doe eyes. She was wearing a dark blue cocktail dress and a pair of killer heels and a bright pink sash that said *Hen Night* across it in big, curly letters. Jack was relieved when he noticed that the petite black-haired woman beside her was wearing the sash that said *bride-to-be*, meaning that the girl with the dazzling smile may very well be available. Jack's grin grew wider and he gave Lewis a mischievous nudge.

"See that girl in the blue dress? Tonight, I'm going to take her home."

"You reckon?" Lewis replied, looking the mysterious woman up and down with interest. "She's attractive, alright. You've got to be careful, though, Jack. You don't want to get snapped going at it again."

Jack laughed out loud. "That was over a year ago."

"Your father hasn't forgotten about it."

"Don't remind me."

Being rich was as good as being famous in Vegas and Jack's father was constantly in the press and, more recently, so was Jack. Yet, where Jack's father was celebrated for his business intuition, innovative graduate schemes and charitable sponsorship deals, Jack was getting a public reputation as a billionaire playboy and it drove his father crazy.

"Just be discreet about it, yeah?" Lewis advised. "Who am I going to hang out with if you get disowned?"

Jack laughed at his friend's teasing. "Don't worry, Lewis. I'll be on my best behavior."

*****

Natalie was getting married. Annaya would be lying if she said the fact didn't make her a little wistful. Growing up, Annaya had always been the beautiful, tall, gorgeous young woman with model good looks and so naturally, everyone had expected her to be the first to bag a husband.

But little Natalie, with her nervous giggle and tendency to be overly-polite was the one who was ready to settle down with a quiet man who was perfect for her. Annaya was pleased for them, but couldn't help but feel a little envy when shopping for that once-in-a-lifetime dress and fawning over a diamond. It was every girl's dream to be a bride, but

Annaya was far from it.

People told her she was high-maintenance, and she guessed it was true, but it wasn't a need for expensive luxuries and designer clothes that made men fall short of her standards, but her desire to find a man who would put her first. Over the years, she'd come second place to football and careers and ex-girlfriends and it had always left her feeling like she needed just a little more.

When Natalie would ask her about when she'd find a nice man, Annaya would always tell her that she was in no rush. She'd rather find a man who'd sweep her off her feet in an incredible romance, than settle for someone who could take her or leave her.

Natalie's husband-to-be, Daniel, treated Natalie like she was the only woman in the world and that's what

Annaya was searching for--a man who would look at her the way Daniel looked at Natalie, like she was higher than gold and diamonds. Annaya wanted that kind of love and was quick to move on from anyone who made her doubt they were anything less than a match made in heaven. That was often her downfall when it came to finding a man. Annaya was impatient. She wouldn't wait for love to grow; there had to be an *instant* spark.

As her early twenties rolled past and then her mid-twenties too, Annaya began to accept that if the love of her life was out there, it may take quite some time to find him. In the meantime, she'd decided, she was going to make the most of what *was* available right here and right now: some good old-fashioned no-strings attached fun.

As all the taken girls gathered together in a group, laughing and giggling and talking about their multiple upcoming weddings, new houses and babies, Annaya let her own eyes subtly sweep over the casino; over the roulette wheel and spin machines, looking to see if there was any way to avoid being the only one to go back to her hotel room alone that night.

Across town, in another casino, Daniel and all his buddies were having their own stag do and all the other girls' partners were with him, which meant that far from being a wild night, the hen party would probably come to an eleven 'o' clock end, followed by all of the couples sitting in the hotel lobby having a quiet drink. Annaya hated being a third wheel when that happened and so was keen to see if there was any potential that night for her to find some company of her own.

Her eyes lit up when she noticed the dark-haired, handsome Italian-looking man who had just walked through the door. He was tall and lean, with slightly arrogant eyes and a very confident grin. Annaya felt a smile creep onto her face and then she had to laugh at herself. Natalie always told her that if she wanted a magical romance, she had to stop fooling around with arrogant men, but Annaya couldn't help it. She just had a thing for bad boys with an ego.

Natalie followed her friend's gaze and rolled her eyes. "Really, Annaya?"

"What?" Annaya said defensively, giving a little laugh. "I know you're all going to couple up later and then what am I meant to do?"

"I've tried to set you up with Daniel's friends, but you said you weren't interested."

"Don't get me wrong, Nat, Daniel is amazing, but his friends are all just a bit..."

"-safe?" Natalie guessed. "That's what you want when you're looking to settle down." The bride-to-be looked Jack over with a critical frown and then gave her friend a concerned look. "Take my word for it, Annaya. That one will be trouble."

Annaya laughed off her concern and gave a nonchalant little shrug. "Maybe he is," she agreed, "but what harm is a little trouble when it's just for one night?"

*****

Jack didn't go to Annaya straight away, even though he'd noticed her looking his way with that interested little smile. No, instead he decided to play the long game and let her wonder. That was part of the fun, he found, of one-night encounters. It was the thrill of looking at a stranger across a crowded room and wondering who they were and where they'd come from.

It was taking the time to speculate whether the stunning girl by the poker table was a demure single girl from some rural town; a devilish wife who liked to flirt with other men; a student gambling away her loan money; or another billionaire's child out to have some fun. It was the guessing that made the hunt feel like a game and Jack liked to draw it out slowly.

Looking at this divine creature, he imagined she was twenty-eight or twenty-nine and by the sharp look in her eyes, he'd have said that she was pretty smart and probably the sort who could hold her own. There were other handsome men in the room – some even trying to catch her eye – but her own eyes kept consistently coming back to him and she wasn't afraid to be caught staring, either.

That made Jack guess that she was something of a tease, or at least not unfamiliar with going after what she wanted. She had a raw sexual appeal that she used expertly, letting a knowing little smile cross her lips when she saw him watching her and leaning over the table to place her chips just a little further across than was needed in order to show off her incredible figure.

"Wow," Lewis chuckled, noticing the intensity building between them from across the casino. "She keeps looking at you."

"She's interesting, isn't she?"

That's the only way Jack knew to describe her, because the way Annaya conducted herself was new to him and it intrigued him greatly. In his experience, woman who owned their sexuality tended to be promiscuous and verging on slutty.

This was not the case with Annaya. Yes, she knew she was attractive and how to move her body in order to draw Jack's eye. But there was a certain grace to her movements; a kind of refinement that stopped her flirtations from ever crossing over into anything that could be described as vulgar.

She wanted him to look, but Jack could also tell this was not a woman who would let a man take control. He felt like he'd met his match and his attraction grew as their glances grew more frequent and fiery.

Annaya was surrounded by other woman in equally

short dresses and high heels, but she stood out from the crowd in every way, from her incredible beauty, to the sound of her laugh, to the way she moved; Jack was enchanted.

He kept his cool for as long as possible, playing a few spins of the wheel with Lewis and throwing down a few chips at this table and the next, but when he saw Annaya moving away from her group towards the bar, he knew it was time to make his move.

"Going after her, hey?" Lewis said knowingly. "Need a wingman?"

"Not tonight, Lewis," Jack grinned. "The way she's been looking at me tonight, she's just waiting for me to go and speak to her."

"Remember what I said," Lewis offered as one final

piece of advice, "don't do anything stupid."

*****

It had been a while since Annaya had flirted the way she did that night, but she couldn't get enough of the look in the handsome stranger's eyes when he stared at her. It was like she was casting a spell over him. She could see it in the way he had started off so cool and casual, like he owned the place, but as the minutes ticked by and she didn't fall at his feet despite him catching her eye, she could see him begin to become intrigued.

He started to make more of an effort to get her attention by placing bigger bets and shaking hands with the best-dressed men and women walking by, as if he knew everyone in town and wanted her to know it.

There were beautiful women in the casino that night; young, gorgeous and dripping in diamonds, but the handsome stranger's steady gaze didn't waver an instant. Annaya loved how empowered it made her feel to know that she could capture his attention that way and she started to use her heavy eyelashes and hourglass figure to her advantage, moving in a way that she knew would be the most alluring.

"Annaya, you just won!"

"Huh?"

Natalie followed Annaya's gaze again and once more rolled her eyes, but her laugh was forgiving. "I've lost you," she said. "You're fawning all over that guy.

You might as well go and get him. We're all going to be heading back to the hotel lobby soon anyway. Go on. You have my blessing. Just take care of yourself and don't do anything stupid, alright?"

Annaya blushed to have been caught swooning over a man all night and she gave Natalie a grateful hug. "I'm sorry, Nat. I know I've been daydreaming all night. I promise to make it up to you at the fitting next week. We'll drink champagne and read bridal magazines and discuss flower arrangements... I'll be all yours, I swear."

"It's fine," Natalie laughed. "Go and have some fun. I'm getting married in a month and God knows you might be the only one of us left with any interesting stories to tell. Go hook up for us married ones and promise to tell us all about it in the morning."

The flirtatious maid-of-honor said goodbye to the girls and, with the bride's permission, made her way casually to the bar. She could have just walked straight over to the handsome stranger, of course, but that would have made it too easy for him. No, she wanted him to come to her.

She separated herself from the group and ordered a glass of wine. Then she sat on that high bar stool with one shapely leg crossed over the other and one hand holding the neck of her glass. She had to resist the urge to keep looking over her shoulder to see if the sexy Italian was coming her way if she wanted to keep hold of her upper hand.

A small smile came to her face when a few moments later, she could feel the heat of someone standing behind her and she heard the sound of a deep, seductive voice saying, "I'll take a glass of the McAllen. Thank you."

Annaya tried not to look impressed when the barman didn't charge the stranger for the drink. She wondered if he came here often enough to have a tab, or whether he was someone more important than she'd realized. The stranger leaned with one elbow against the bar and turned to look at her with devilish eyes and a seductive smile.

"It's not often a woman intrigues me enough to take me away from a poker game. So, tell me, what's the name of the most beautiful woman in Vegas?"

Annaya let out a little laugh at the chat-up line which would have sounded so cheesy coming from anyone else, but made her heart flutter when coming from him. "Annaya."

"It's a pleasure to meet you, Annaya. My name is Jack. Now, I'm wondering if those friends of yours would mind at all if I stole you away, because I would really like to take you out tonight."

Annaya felt her heart begin to beat quickly in her chest from her attraction to him and the excitement of having him stand so close to her with the offer to take her out that night made adrenaline pump through her veins. It felt so dangerous and so unexpected to agree to go off with a man she knew nothing about, but her body wouldn't let her say "no" even if her head told her to be cautious.

His smile was too charming and his eyes too alluring for her to be afraid, so it was only with a little hesitation that Annaya looked back over her shoulder at her friends one last time, before looking up to catch Jack's deep, dark eyes and smile. "I'm all yours."

*

Annaya's head was pounding. She couldn't remember the last time she'd had that much to drink. In fact, it would be fair to say she didn't remember last night at all. It was all a blur of spinning wheels and jackpots and bells and laughter. She let her eyes slowly flicker open and although everything was something of a hazy blur, she was able to recognize the golden covers of her own hotel room bed and the bedside table covered in the jewelry she'd thrown off.

She could see last night's pair of heels thrown aside on the carpet and her blue dress over the back of a chair. She realized then she was completely naked under the covers and giggled at herself for having a wild night. She couldn't wait to meet up again with Natalie and find out what had happened. The morning-after stories were always the best.

She let out a little yelp of surprise when she heard a groan emanating from beside her and then felt the body of a man rolling over and sitting up beside her. Annaya's surprised eyes caught with Jack's and she let out a gasp to match his amused laugh. It was only now that she laid eyes on him, that Annaya vaguely remembered flirtatiously leaning over a poker table to draw the attention of a handsome stranger from across the bar and how he'd offered to take her out.

They'd stayed at the bar for two or three more drinks after that offer, and after that, the night began to become a bit patchy. Annaya sort of remembered going dancing and she sort of remembered being at a neon-covered building with a steeple of some sort. The most vivid memories amongst the drunken haze were those that had been made in this very bed.

The naked woman looked down at her shoes again and remembered kicking them off before Jack had powerfully pulled her close and pressed his lips down over hers. She could recall the *zweep* of her cocktail dress zip being pulled down by his strong hands and she even remembered the sensation of his hands running over her waist. With a sudden jolt, she remembered they'd made love last night. The memory made her blush deeply and pull the covers up over her chest, but when she turned to look again at Jack, she could see that he was still grinning.

"Are you not used to drinking that much?" he asked her kindly, but with a slightly teasing tone under his words.

"Not in recent years."

"Do you remember what happened last night?"

"Did we... I mean... we had...?"

"We did. And it was good, if I remember rightly, although I'll admit that there are some blanks from last night. I don't even remember how we got back to the hotel."

"Me neither."

"Safe to say we had a good night. Are you alright?"

Annaya nodded numbly and then allowed herself a little chuckle. She'd been surprised to find Jack in her bed, but she remembered now just how desperate she had been to bring him back here and how her heart had skipped a beat the minute she first saw him. It was still fluttering now at the sight of him.

He was also naked beneath the sheets, but sitting up, Annaya could see the toned muscles of his abdomen and strong shoulders. It made her feel a sudden surge of lust all over again and she almost wanted to kiss him and recreate the events of the night before, but Jack was already standing up and searching for his clothes.

"How long are you in town for?" he asked her, as he pulled on his dress shirt and black pants.

"We're going back today."

"Where are you from?"

"Bakersfield, California."

"Shame. I'd have liked to see you again."

Annaya watched him get dressed and felt sorry that it would all be over so quickly. She couldn't remember the last time a man had quite got her blood pumping like that, but she had no regrets. She had wanted some no-strings attached fun and that was just what she was getting. The worst thing about their one-night stand was the burning curiosity that Annaya was left with about the man.

Who was he? What did he do? He'd had had all the charm and lines of James Bond, but Annaya wouldn't have known if he was just a casino waiter. She supposed it was best to let the mystery remain and have fond memories of a wild night instead of driving herself mad wondering just who she'd slept with.

She leaned forward onto her knees and watched him get dressed. Her expression became concerned when she saw Jack stop when he noticed a little bundle of papers on the side and saw his expression become confused. She had no idea what the papers were, but she could see from the way his mouth had fallen open slightly that they were shocking to him.

"What is it?"

"These are photos."

Annaya began to giggle. She wondered if one of them had taken some cheeky snaps of their bedtime antics and now Jack was shocked by their night together. She held out her hand eagerly.

"Let me see!"

Jack's face was serious as he handed over the pictures and when Annaya began to flip through them, her own face became serious too. These were no kinky shots of naked bodies. No, these were pictures of two strangers very unmistakably getting married. There she was, in her blue cocktail dress with a huge grin on her face, holding a little bouquet in one hand and with her other arm linked with Jack's. In the picture, he was also grinning wildly and they were standing in front of a cheesy Vegas chapel covered in neon lights.

That's why Annaya remembered neon and steeples... She flicked through to the next picture, hoping that she'd be able to reason all this away and find that they'd just gate-crashed somebody else's elopement. She had no such luck. Right there was a picture, clear as day, of her and Jack signing a very official-looking marriage license.

A shocked hand flew to her mouth and as her gaze flew around the room again for any further evidence of her misdemeanor, she noticed a 'Just Married' sign swinging from the frame at the bottom of the bed and spotted a corsage amongst her jewelry on the side.

"This can't be real."

"It looks real to me. Do you remember any of that?"

"Neon."

"Bloody neon. I can't believe this is happening." Jack began to pace the room frantically with his hands in his hair and shook his head in furious disbelief. Suddenly he turned on his heel and pointed frenziedly in Annaya's direction. "You can't tell *anyone* about this. Ever. I'm going to make it go away."

"How arc you going to do that?"

"We'll get an annulment. Immediately."

"Alright."

"This is a mess."

"Calm down. We'll get an annulment."

Annaya began to giggle again. She'd always been known as the wild one in her group of friends, but this was crazy even for her. Yet, even though she knew this whole thing was mad, she couldn't help but see the funny side of falling into that rom-com cliché of a drunken Vegas marriage. Natalie had wanted a story and she wouldn't be disappointed!

"It's not funny," Jack said sullenly. "This is just the sort of thing that could be the final straw for me."

"What do you mean?"

"I've been treading on thin ice with my father for a while now. If he gets wind of this, he'll publicly disown me and I'll be out on the streets."

"And how's your father going to find out?" Annaya

37

said calmly. "He wasn't there, was he?"

"He didn't have to be."

Jack stepped over to the window furtively, like a criminal on the run, and pulled back the curtain to look down at the street outside. Annaya saw him breathe a sigh of relief and he turned back over his shoulder to explain things a little more.

"My father is Brandon Casali."

"Is that meant to mean something to me?"

"Casali. Like Casali Casinos. He's worth billions. If you were from Nevada you'd know his name. Take a look."

Jack picked up a newspaper, which had been laid down on the coffee table by the hotel staff and threw it over to the bed. Annaya picked it up and her eyes widened when she saw that Brandon Casali's new development project was front page news of the local paper.

"If we got papped last night, then our pictures could be all over the front of tomorrow's paper. That would not go down well."

"Well, fix it!" Annaya interjected quickly. Suddenly the situation seemed a lot more serious and she felt panic setting in. What had been a fun story to tell her friends and a bit of hassle in the form of paperwork, would be a lot more of an issue. It could mean her face in a national paper with people laughing at her for her drunken mistakes. "Jesus, Jack. Why didn't you tell me last night? If I'd have known you were such a big shot, maybe I'd have..."

"--have what?" Jack interrupted. He gave her a stern and knowing look and Annaya shut her mouth. They both knew that even if she had known about his inheritance that nothing would have happened any differently. The moment they'd laid eyes on each other, they'd been destined to end up here. It was magnetism.

Annaya swung her legs over the side of the bed and stood up with the sheets still wrapped around her. She began to follow Jack around the room as he picked up his socks from one corner of the hotel suite and his shoes from another. Eventually, he turned around to face her and let out a patient sigh. He brought her to a stand-still with two reassuring hands on her shoulders and told her he would deal with it.

"I can get this sorted," he vowed, "but I'm going to

need your signature, so don't go anywhere. Stay in this hotel. I'll be back as soon as I can with everything we need to make this go away."

With that, he was gone and Annaya felt deflated. She remembered just how excited she'd been last night when she'd locked eyes with the sexiest man she'd ever seen and how her heart had fluttered when he'd asked if he could steal her for the night. She'd been so looking forward to a fun and carefree night, but now it all felt like more of a nightmare. She felt like Jack was angry with her and like the whole world was watching.

Still, she couldn't help but marvel at the night's events. How had she managed to seduce a billionaire? The thought was ludicrous and just as quickly as she'd felt dismayed, she felt the laughter bubbling up again.

It was just absurd, wasn't it? she thought. Luckily for Jack, Annaya wasn't a gold-digger and had no interest in denying an annulment for the sake of a hefty divorce settlement, although she did wonder what it would be like to be that mind-blowingly rich. She guessed it was just another fantasy to push to the back of her mind, just like her fantasy of having one incredible night that didn't end in tears.

Chapter 2

There was a little cheer from all the girls sitting in the hotel breakfast bar when Annaya entered and she bowed her head in shame and scurried to her seat at the head of the table next to Natalie, who looked well rested and excited.

"So?" her friend urged, taking a large bite of a jam-covered croissant. "Did you end up having to sleep alone?"

"Oh God, Natalie, I've done something so stupid!"

Natalie leaned forward with interest and lowered her voice so that the other girls wouldn't overhear them. "What have you done?"

"I drank too much and went to a chapel with Jack..."

"No. *No. No!*" Natalie's voice became gradually louder as she put two and two together and then she gasped. "You married that guy?"

"Ssh! Keep your voice down. He's gone to the courthouse. We're going to get it annulled."

"Dear God, Annaya! You don't even know who he is!"

"He's loaded. I know that much."

"What do you mean?"

"You know that casino we were in last night? His father owns it."

"You're joking!"

"I'm dead serious. Apparently, he's the son of a billionaire and this morning he freaked out thinking that the press were onto us. According to him, it's one more slip-up and his father will disown him."

"Oh my God..." Natalie gasped again. "Well, nobody can say that you don't deliver when you promise a story."

"What am I going to do, Nat? I feel awful. My head's pounding, my mouth's dry and somewhere out in Vegas there's a billionaire who's pretty annoyed with me."

"It takes two for something like that to happen, Annaya. He was throwing just as many glances as you last night."

"I hardly remember."

"You couldn't take your eyes off each other."

"Oh God, Natalie. I just want this to go away. I don't want to end up in the paper. Everyone will say that I'm a gold-digger or after my five minutes of fame. I just want to keep my head down and get as far away from him as soon as possible."

"Get some coffee in you," Natalie advised, "You look awful. Calm yourself down. Everything's going to be OK. If he's got that sort of money, then he's sure to be able to pull some strings."

"You're right. I'm so sorry, Nat. I didn't mean to cause a scene at your hen-do. I promise that as soon as we're back in California, I'm going to be as good as gold."

Natalie let out a light little laugh and raised her

eyebrows with amusement. "I highly doubt that, but it's alright. You wouldn't be you without leaving a trail of drama everywhere you go."

It was true. Annaya had been a bit of a livewire during her youth. She didn't mean to cause trouble. It was just that she had an irrepressible spontaneous streak that she found impossible to ignore.

At prom, she'd been the one to break her wrist trying to climb up onto the stage to dance and at their high school graduation, she'd been the one to trip on her own gown and fall on her face. Then there had been that night, out where a bar fight had started when two men had both tried to hit on her at once. And one could not forget that quiet trip to the shore that had ended in disaster when Annaya had been certain that she knew how to drive a jet-ski.

She never went out with the intention of having something dramatic happen, but she always seemed to be the one with the crazy story the next morning and she had something of a reputation now.

Perhaps that's why she and Jack had been so naturally drawn to one another. They were both the young and restless type who loved to live life to the full, even if it meant screwing up every now and then. Well, they'd screwed up this time!

Annaya finished breakfast and tried to look innocent in front of the other girls and their partners as they all drank orange juice and nibbled on toast. Annaya's head was still spinning from the night before and she could hardly face eating anything, but she didn't want anyone to question her about what she'd got up to after she'd left the casino, so she tried to play it off as if she'd had a quiet night.

All the same, her thoughts kept drifting back to the self-assured, sexy Jack Casali and they weren't thoughts of panic. No, she found herself daydreaming about his broad shoulders and charming smile and wishing that her memories of the night before weren't so clouded. If only there was a way to live the night again and to recall every sensation in perfect detail.

After breakfast, Annaya did as she was told and returned to her hotel room to wait for Jack. Her flight was leaving in just a few hours and she began to get agitated as she waited for his return, not wanting to miss it and then have to travel alone. She felt a surge of relief rush over her when he rushed into the hotel room just thirty minutes or so later with a file of documents in his hand.

He'd gotten changed since that morning and was wearing a pair of smart pants and a blue shirt. His hair, which had been ruffled that morning, had been neatly combed back and his clothes were perfectly ironed. He looked the picture of innocence and nothing like the chuckling one-night stand he'd appeared that morning. He came into the room slightly breathless from rushing and breathed a sigh of relief when he saw Annaya waiting for him on the sofa in the suite.

"Great! You're still here."

"Did you get everything we need?"

"Yes. I just need you to sign these papers."

"Got a pen?"

Jack handed her a pen and the forms and laid them

down in front of her on the little coffee table. Annaya quickly flicked through the pages, signing her name on every dotted line until she got to the last page and then she breathed her own sigh of relief and handed the paperwork back to Jack.

"Thank you for handling this so well," he told her. "I know I rushed out of here in kind of a panic this morning, but I guess it was a shock for you too."

"I'm just glad it can be sorted."

"It will. My lawyer assures me that he'll be able to rush this through. With any luck, it will be annulled within days."

"Let me give you my number," Annaya said, scrawling down her digits on the back of Jack's hand. "Give me a call when it's all gone through. Just in case I want to elope with someone else in the meantime."

Jack let out a little laugh that was tired, but relieved. "It was kind of a crazy night, but I'd be lying if I said I didn't have fun. If you're ever in Vegas again, come by the casino. I'll take you out for a night that doesn't end in nuptials."

"That sounds good to me."

They said their final goodbyes and Jack helped Annaya carry her suitcase to the elevator and then rode down with her to the hotel lobby where the other girls were already gathered with their cases. They began to giggle and gossip when they saw Jack holding Annaya's case and Annaya turned red, ready for the onslaught of questions that would ensue. Jack simply gave the women a small smile and then turned to give Annaya one final, reserved peck on the cheek.

"Safe flight."

"Thanks."

Then the billionaire turned on his heel and was gone. All the girls began to squeal and flocked around Annaya with interest.

"Who was that?"

"Did you sleep with him?"

"Did you get his number?"

"Are you going to see him again?"

Annaya waved away their questions with her hand and gave a nonchalant smile and a casual, coy shrug. "It was just a one-night stand, girls."

"That's a shame," one of the girls, Amy, commented. "He was gorgeous."

"He was, wasn't he?" Annaya agreed. She and Natalie exchanged knowing smiles and fell to the back of the pack to walk to the cab that had come to pick them up to take them to the airport.

"How'd it go?" Natalie asked quietly.

"Fine. He said it would be annulled within days."

"Are you alright?"

"Why shouldn't I be?"

"I don't know. I guess that was just a bit of a rollercoaster ride, even for you."

"It's just another story to tell, Nat."

Annaya brushed off the whole event as though it didn't matter, but inside she did feel a little sad. She was always that girl that men slept with, but never the one that they called the next day. She was the girl who always had a great story to tell, but never the one who could hold a man's attention for long. She felt a sudden awareness of everything that was missing in her life.

Sure, she loved getting attention from men and for the most part, she enjoyed the freedom of being single and the excitement of knowing that she could have any man she wanted. Every night out was a potential opportunity for a romantic affair and a new sexual encounter.

Annaya had to confess that she was starting to grow tired of the revolving door of men in her life.

Wouldn't it really be something new to be with one guy for a reasonable length of time? Wouldn't it be something to fall in love and settle down and follow in the steps of all her girlfriends who had managed to find a single man to be with forever?

The feeling of being lonely was one that Annaya wouldn't let herself feel very often, but it was there all the same. It was difficult now that all of her friends had coupled up and were settling down. She simultaneously longed for those wild days of partying and being totally uninhibited as one of a group of single girls and was envious of her friends who'd moved past all that and found something that meant more to them than a fun night.

What was Annaya doing with her life? As she flew home and then took the train back to her own apartment in Bakersfield, she told herself that it was time to make a new commitment to being serious. No more one-night stands. No more fleeting sexual encounters. Jack would be her last wild fling.

It was late by the time that Annaya made it home to her cozy little apartment and she was glad to be able to finally put her feet up and fall back on her bed. She felt exhausted and decided to leave her bag unpacked until the morning, although she did root around in her purse to check her phone. It had been turned off during the flight and she was surprised to find when she flicked it back on, that she had one new voicemail. She listened to it curiously.

The voice on the other end of the line was that of Jack Casali. "Hi Annaya. It's Jack. I just wanted to say sorry again for everything that happened last night and how I handled it. I really meant it when I said it was a shame that you wouldn't be sticking around. You're a beautiful woman."

There was a pause then, as though the confident playboy didn't know what to say and so he quickly changed the topic back to the matter-at-hand. "I'll let you know when the papers go through and in the meantime, please don't tell anyone what happened. Word gets out easy.

"I guess that's all. It was nice meeting you. Bye."

Annaya half-laughed at the awkward voicemail and plugged her cell in to charge, threw off her clothes and crawled beneath the covers. She couldn't help but notice how quiet it was in Bakersfield compared to Vegas and she began to wonder again about the kind of night she'd really had with Jack.

She thought about how it would be nice to have someone with her right now. Still, she decided not to dwell on it. After all, she'd managed to take home the most eligible bachelor in Vegas. Wasn't that some story?

One day, when she was settled down with her husband – a nice, quiet man – she would once again tell stories of her wild youth and they would all laugh about it and how much she had changed. For now, she pulled her covers more tightly around her and pressed her eyes shut, beginning to dream of roulette wheels and dark eyes before she'd even fallen asleep.

*****

"So, what happened with the girl after you'd taken off the other night?"

Jack and Lewis were having drinks at an upscale bar in the center of Vegas. It had been almost three days since Annaya got on a plane and flown away, but Jack still couldn't get her off of his mind. It must have shown, because Lewis was asking more questions than usual. Jack raised his eyebrows in a cross between amusement and exasperation when he recalled all that had happened in one night with Annaya and smiled.

"Remember how you told me to stay out of trouble?"

"That sounds ominous."

"We ended up in some God-awful neon chapel. I woke up in her bed the next morning and found photos of the marriage."

Jack had expected shock or admonition from Lewis,

but instead, his friend melted into laughter and gave Jack a brotherly, teasing shove. "How on earth do you get yourself into these situations, Jack? What did you drink?"

"I don't even know," Jack confessed, giving into his own laughter now. "I don't remember a thing we did that night after we left the casino."

"The last I saw of you, you were getting pretty close at the bar. Then you put your arm around her and walked out. So, what are you going to do about the marriage?"

"The papers for an annulment have already been filed. I should be in the clear in just a few days."

"She didn't fight it at all? Try and get a settlement?"

Jack smiled. "She didn't even know who I was, even

when I told her – not a flicker. She just didn't want to be in the papers, I think."

"Are you going to see her again?"

"She's flown back to Bakersfield."

"So? That's what private jets are for."

The billionaire's son laughed again. "I think it's best to put it behind me and lie low for a while. I was terrified the next day that I would find it all over the papers. If word ever gets back to my father, then I certainly want to make sure it's at a time when I'm in his good books."

"That's a shame," Lewis said. "You've not seemed that interested in a woman in a long time."

"She was pretty incredible, wasn't she?"

The conversation ended and the two wealthy heirs went their separate ways. As the chauffeur drove him home, all Jack could think about was how amazing Annaya had been. A smile came to his face every time that he imagined her in that navy dress, shooting flirty glances his way across a poker table.

Lewis was right. It had been a long time since a woman had truly captured his attention. After all, his fortune meant that woman came easily.

Unfortunately, they tended to be a certain type of woman – shallow, conceited, predictable. Annaya had been something different – free-spirited, seductive, spontaneous. Jack thought about the message he'd left for her on her answering machine and wondered if he should have said more.

No, he decided at last. It was best to let one fun night

remain one fun night. In his experience, the trouble with women always began the morning after.

Chapter3

Annaya stared at the little blue line and her legs began to tremble. She thought back to her one night with Jack and her memories were too hazy to remember if there had been a condom amongst all the neon lights and champagne. Yet, six weeks after her one-night-stand with the billionaire, she'd found that her body was telling her that something had changed and there was only one thing that it could be. Now, a pregnancy test confirmed her worst fears and she slowly sat down on the edge of the bath to gather her thoughts as her head began to spin.

She was pregnant by the son of a billionaire casino tycoon and he lived in the playboy capital of the world. When she tried to think of any way that everything was going to turn out alright, she just kept coming back to the fact that someone like Jack would never be there for someone like her. Of course, Natalie was the first to know. Annaya invited her friend over for a cup of tea and it was only when the bride-to-be was sitting down that Annaya felt that she could break the news.

"Hey Nat," she began, trying to sound casual. Her friend's eyes immediately narrowed with suspicion, knowing Annaya too well to believe that any sentence that began with "Hey Nat'' would be innocent.

"Yes?"

"You remember that one-night stand I had in Vegas?"

"With the billionaire and the elopement? Yes. I vaguely recall."

"Well, it turns out that everything didn't go away as neatly as I'd hoped."

"The marriage didn't get annulled?"

"No. Something else."

"Oh my God, Annaya. You're pregnant, aren't you? Bloody typical! Drama just follows you everywhere you go. Tell me everything."

"I was late and I kept waiting, thinking that it would come and then I started thinking about that night with Jack and thought I better check. Three pregnancy tests down and I don't think there's any doubt left."

"Geez. So, what are you going to do? Have you told him yet?"

"No. Do you think I should?" Annaya bit down on her

lip anxiously and began to fiddle with a strand of her curly hair.

"Why would you even question it, Annaya? Of course you need to tell him. Why wouldn't you?"

"Because of who he is. What if he thinks I'm just making it up to get something out of him? Or worse still, what if I go to him for help and he just shrugs me off? There's no way he's going to give up Vegas to come here, so what's even the point of bothering him?"

"Are you serious? Annaya, you're carrying his child. That's not something you keep to yourself. Maybe he'll be there, maybe he won't, but either way, he's got to know."

"You're right," Annaya sighed, burying her head in

her hands. "I just don't want him to think I planned it this way."

"Let him think what he likes. You're no gold-digger. He'll have met enough to know. Trust me."

"What should I do? Just call him?"

"Call him."

"I will."

"Go on then."

"Tonight."

Natalie gave her friend a stern look and sighed. "Fine. Tonight. But don't chicken out, Annaya. You need to tell him what's going on. And then tell me what he says."

Annaya felt better after talking to Natalie, who felt sorry for her best friend since childhood. It always seemed that Annaya was the one in the spotlight, jumping from one crisis to the next, while Natalie was the calm and steady rock who kept Annaya anchored in real life. God knew she needed Natalie now.

Annaya was good at hiding it, but she was in a state of shock. Never in a million years would she ever have expected to have found herself pregnant to a stranger at the age of twenty-nine. Of course, she'd always been a bit wild, but she'd expected all that to fade away when she met the right man and settled down. Now, all her plans were in disarray. Who'd take on a single mom in her thirties? Jack Casali?

*****

Jack was surprised to see Annaya's name flashing on

his smartphone when the cell began to ring. He assumed she was calling to chase him up about the annulment and so he quickly answered. It surprised him how exciting he found even the sound of her voice and he answered with a confident, "Annaya. Good evening. What can I do for you?"

The voice of the woman on the other end, so flirtatious and sexy that fateful night, now serious, and that immediately made Jack take a seat at his office desk.

"Hi Jack. I'm sorry to be calling you out of the blue, but something's come up."

"What is it?"

"I'm pregnant."

"Pregnant? Are you sure?"

"Positive."

"Is it mine?"

"Of course it's yours! There's been nobody else."

Jack felt his stomach drop and ice run through his veins. He immediately envisioned word of this getting out to his father and his inheritance being ripped away as he was sent away in shame. He knew he had to step up to the mark and help Annaya, but he wanted to do it quietly. He sighed heavily.

"I'll come and see you," he promised. "We'll figure something out. Can you keep the news to yourself until we've had a chance to speak?"

Annaya sighed irritably. She wasn't too impressed that she had Jack's baby growing inside her and his main concern was making sure nobody found out.

Still, his offer to come and see her to discuss things was already more than she'd expected from him, so after letting out a long breath, she answered curtly, "Fine."

"Thank you. I'll be there tomorrow. What's your address?"

Annaya reeled off her details and Jack wrote them down. Afterwards, there was a long and painful pause on the line when neither knew what to say. The distance between them made the situation all the more uncomfortable. Jack wasn't always the most emotional or vocal man, but at least if he'd been with her, he'd have been able to take hold of her hand and give it a squeeze of reassurance. As it was, he simple found himself clearing his throat after the silence had continued too long and reiterating that he'd be there the next day.

"Try not to worry about it, OK? I'll sort it out."

*****

"He said he'd sort it out."

"'Sort it out'? What the hell does that mean?"

"God knows if I know, Nat!"

"It sounds like he's going to send a hit man your way. Jesus."

"It seems to be his way. He said the same thing after finding out about the marriage. 'I'll sort it out'."

"Typical. Although, I suppose at least he's agreed to come and see you. That's something, isn't it?"

"I think he's just worried I'm going to say something

to someone."

"So what? Nobody here knows who he is."

"I suppose it only takes one person to wonder if there's a story in it for it to get out," Annaya sighed. "I don't want it in the press either."

"What are you going to say to him when he comes? Are you going to keep it?"

"I don't know, Nat. I don't think I could get rid of it. That's just not me. Besides, I'm almost thirty. Will I get another chance to have kids?"

Annaya could almost hear Nat's pity emanating down the line when she spoke about her time running out and her friend's voice became gentler in reply. "You've got to make the right decision for you, Annaya. You're a catch. You'll meet the right one."

"We've been saying that for years. Besides, I think I'd be a good mom. Man or no."

"Of course you would. You'd be the best mom. But do you really want to do that on your own?"

"No, not really. But if I have to, I will."

"Whatever you do, you know I'll support you, but just go in with your eyes open, Annaya. It wouldn't be easy on your own."

"I'll see what Jack says when he gets here."

"When does he come?"

"Tomorrow."

"Do you want me to be there with you?"

"No. Thanks, Nat. I'll be OK. Besides, you've got

more important things to focus on! You're getting married in a month! Seriously, I'll be fine."

"Well, you know where I am if you need me."

"Thanks, Nat."

Annaya put the phone down and felt her stomach doing little nervous flips. She'd known she was pregnant for a couple of days, but the reality of it hadn't really hit her until she'd called Jack, and now that she'd just spoken to Natalie, the harsh truth of the matter seemed even more real.

Tomorrow, she'd see the sexy Jack Casali again and that sent waves of nervousness coursing through her. What would he say? Would he try and convince her to get rid of it? Would he pay her for her silence? Annaya couldn't help but fear the worst. After all, she'd only known Jack for one night and she hardly remembered any of that time. The man was a stranger with a high profile. What did that mean for Annaya and her baby?

Chapter4

Annaya opened the door and immediately, her breath caught in her throat. Jack was even more handsome than she remembered him. Today he was wearing a smart, grey suit that was tailored to fit every perfect dimension of his sculpted body and his dark hair was combed back. He had just a day's stubble on his cheek, which gave his otherwise chic appearance a slightly rugged look that made Annaya weak at the knees. When she opened the door, he met her eyes and smiled.

"Hello."

"Hi."

"Can I come in?"

"Sure."

Annaya felt slightly embarrassed to let Jack into her tiny little apartment with its cracks in the plaster and old, sagging sofa. She imagined that he never spent time in places as modest as hers and although she'd made sure it was clean and tidy, she was still painfully aware of how small and cramped it must seem in comparison to a mansion and how scruffy all the possessions that she'd owned forever.

She led him into the kitchen and he lingered by the doorway as she set the kettle boiling to make coffee in her old, chipped mugs. They made small talk as she bustled around, both waiting for the moment to be right before they began to address the real reason why Jack was there.

"Nice place. I didn't get to ask you what you do, last

time we were together."

"Yeah. I guess we didn't get much chance to chat, did we? Well, I'm an office assistant. Exciting, huh?"

"An office assistant? That surprises me."

"What did you think I'd do?"

"Something crazier than that."

"Something more Vegas?"

Jack smiled at that and leaned against the counter casually, letting his eyes run over all the trinkets in her kitchen and the photo of her and Natalie on the wall. He pointed to the picture of the petite bride-to-be.

"She was with you that night, right?"

Annaya looked over her shoulder to see what he was looking at. She smiled. "That's Natalie, my best friend. We were in Vegas for her hen night. She gets married in a month."

"And you? Are you single?"

The hostess let out a little laugh and gave him a slightly questioning look. "What do you think of me? 'Are you single?,' 'Is it mine?'."

Jack let out a little chuckle. "I'm sorry," he apologized. "It's just I don't know you all that well."

"I guess it wasn't the best first impression," Annaya admitted.

She handed Jack his coffee and led him to the sitting room. They both sat down on the sofa and leaned back to talk. Annaya was finding it hard to catch his eye. Every time she did, she thought back to their night together and the half-formed memories of their naked bodies intertwined, or else, she thought of the giant elephant in the room that neither of them was ready to face. More than that, she found his sex appeal disarming and it made it difficult for her to focus on the things they really needed to discuss.

"And how about you? Are you single?"

"Yes."

"Recently single?"

"Long-term single," Jack told her. "I mean, I've met women. I've taken them out. Spent nights with them. But a relationship? No. I'm something of a lone wolf. How about you? Was there a guy?"

"There have been guys. Nothing has stuck, though."

"So, should we talk about what I'm here to talk about?"

Annaya shot him a slightly annoyed look. She'd have preferred that he'd have let the small talk last just slightly longer so that she'd feel less like a stranger to him when they began to discuss the big questions that were looming over them.

She didn't like the way that he was approaching this like a business deal, but she supposed she couldn't complain. They'd both known that their night together had been a one-night stand, so she reasoned that it wasn't fair of her to expect false formalities now. Down to business it was.

"Alright. Tell me what you're thinking."

"It's not my choice."

"I want to keep it."

Jack took in a short, sharp intake of breath at that and Annaya could see him mulling over her words. He leaned back in his chair and placed his hands on his knees, thinking hard about something. Annaya put her coffee down on the table in front of them and turned to face him. Finally, she caught those dark eyes and that spark that was undeniably between them ignited once more, so that it took her a moment longer to get her words out than she'd expected.

"I'm not after your money or my five minutes of fame," she assured him. "I'm not expecting you to drop everything and play house with me here or for you to put me up in Vegas to be near you. Really, Jack, I'm expecting nothing. I just wanted you to know."

"If you decide to have this baby, then you'll have my support," Jack promised her. "I'll pay for anything you need. I'll make sure you and the baby are taken care of."

Annaya held up her hands to object and shook her head. "I want nothing," she reiterated. "Child support and things for the baby, fine. The rest I'll sort out myself. I'm not looking for a free ride."

"Alright," Jack nodded. "I guess that's that, then. You just need to call me for anything you need. There's just one more thing."

"What do you need?"

"It's awkward to ask but I really need you to keep this quiet. No press."

"I told you: I'm not after making a name for myself.

You don't have to worry about me selling a story. I won't even tell anyone who got me pregnant."

Jack looked down at his lap as though he were ashamed at what he was asking, but then he looked up at Annaya with a grateful smile and gave her hand a reassuring squeeze. "I'm sorry that this has been such a nightmare."

"We should've been more careful, but never mind. What's done is done. I just wanted to get on the same page."

"Sure. Well, whatever happens, I'll make sure you've got everything you need."

"Thanks."

An awkward pause filled the room as what had needed to be discussed had been discussed. There was nothing more to be said to fill the silence

between a man and a woman who were barely more

than strangers.

"Are you flying home tonight?" Annaya asked at last,

just for something to say to break the tension.

"Tomorrow."

"Where are you staying tonight?"

"A hotel, I guess."

"Really? I have a spare room, you know. You could

stay here if you like. It looks like our paths are going

to be crossing again, so it's probably worth getting to

know each other."

Annaya could sense Jack's hesitation as he weighed

up his options and then finally, he nodded. "Alright.

Thanks. My case is in my rental car. I'll go grab it."

Jack left the apartment to go to his rental car downstairs and grab his things. While he was gone, Annaya raced into her bedroom to check that everything was in order. She knew that it was scandalous of her to think that anything would happen between them again tonight, especially with everything that was going on between them, but if things did end up in the bedroom, she at least wanted the bed to be made. By the time Jack returned, she was sitting innocently on the sofa, as though she'd never got up.

"Are you hungry?" she asked. "I can order in."

"Sure."

The hostess pulled out a pile of take-away menus

from the drawer under her TV and they ordered some Chinese food. She poured Jack a glass of wine to help lift the tension in the air and she turned on the television. It was a strange situation. Simultaneously, she felt awkward around the father of her child to-be and incredibly turned on. Even as he sat on the opposite side of the sofa from her, Annaya kept finding her eyes wandering away from the screen to his dark eyes and strong shoulders.

She remembered how lonely she'd felt the night she'd returned from Vegas and crawled into an empty bed and once again the urge to lie with someone else struck her again. Now more than ever, the future felt scary and nothing made her feel safer when everything was falling apart, than to be wrapped up in the arms of a man.

As if reading her mind, Jack turned to her suddenly and asked, "Are you worried about it?"

"The pregnancy? Sure, but I know I'll be alright. How do you feel about it?"

"I'm still struggling to get my head around it, to be honest. I was bowled over when you called. I hadn't been expecting it."

"I'm sorry to have dropped it on you like that."

"No. You were right to call. The last thing I'd want is some journalist turning up asking why a billionaire isn't taking care of the destitute mother of his child..."

Annaya let out a laugh at Jack's warped priorities and she rolled her eyes. "I'm not destitute. God, your reputation matters to you a lot, doesn't it?"

"Not mine, my father's," Jack corrected her. "I'm meant to be a representation of him and I don't do a great job at it."

"You get in trouble a lot, then?"

"I've been told more than once that I have more money than sense. It's probably true."

"So, what do you do? I mean, do you work for your father or have your own job?"

"I'm learning the business," Jack told her. "I'm finding I'm very good with the politics and not so good with the paperwork. All the shaking hands and galas – no problem, but ask me to keep track of the finances and I'm useless. My father would like me to inherit the business when he passes, but I've been told I'm treading on thin ice."

"So, why don't you calm down a bit, if you're pushing your luck?"

A wicked little grin appeared on Jack's face and he met her eye devilishly. "I just like having fun a little too much." He noticed Annaya raising her eyebrows in judgment and he laughed. "Don't give me that look. I'm pretty sure you're the one who suggested getting married."

Annaya laughed. She could tell he was teasing. "I'm sure that was your idea."

"Hmm. I guess we'll have to put it down to a shared moment of madness."

"It was mad, wasn't it?"

The two found themselves laughing and Annaya finally felt some of the tension lift. Yes, the situation was not what either of them had expected. Yes, there were some tricky hurdles ahead, but thank God they could laugh at the madness that had brought them here and try to find some common ground in their shared tendency to take a good time too far.

"It was you who began it," Jack accused her, with a teasing glance. He took a sip of the wine she'd poured him, while Annaya admired the beautiful curve of his neck when he threw his head back to drink.

"Me?"

"You and the way you were leaning across that poker table."

"You were the one who said you wanted to take me out that night."

"You were the one who'd already booked a hotel

94

room."

Annaya gave a wicked grin to match the one that Jack had produced only moments earlier. "I hate being a third wheel to couples."

"Tell me about it. My father has been begging me to get married for years. He thinks the love of a good woman will help me settle down."

"I don't think ours was the kind of marriage he had in mind."

Jack gave her a sideways glance and another mischievous grin. "I could do worse. Oh, that reminds me..." The billionaire opened his case and pulled out some paperwork, which he handed to her. "It came just before I set off this morning. The annulment went through."

"You know, this is how I always imagined my family life would begin," Annaya joked, accepting the papers and laying them down on the side, but there was just a hint of sadness in her voice. No, she hadn't expected the birth of her first child to begin with the annulment of a seedy elopement with his absent father. It was hard for Annaya to accept that nothing had gone according to plan.

Jack reached out and laid a hand on her knee. "I'm going to take care of you," he repeated sincerely. "I really don't want you to worry."

Annaya turned away from him with a sigh and looked down at her lap. "I always thought that I'd be married and settled down with a man before I had kids. I've always looked forward to having someone to come home to, you know? I just hate sleeping alone."

The pregnant woman was surprised when she turned to look back up and the billionaire caught her with a kiss. She gasped and jumped back. "Jack!" she exclaimed. "What are you doing?"

Jack pulled back quickly and apologized. "I'm sorry. I don't know what came over me."

Annaya knew what had come over him. It was the same thing that had come over her. It was the presence of a wild attraction between them and the knowledge that the damage had already been done, so they might as well enjoy each other. Common sense told her that she should politely ask him to leave and sensibly start planning her child's college fund. The woman inside her told her that she didn't know when she'd next be able to share a night with a man, especially one as sexy as Jack.

It wouldn't be too long until her belly grew and then she'd become a single mom and she knew that her opportunities to indulge that wild, sexy side of herself would become few and far between. Why not give in just one last time? Besides, she didn't even remember the first time they'd had sex and she *desperately* wanted to know what it felt like to make love to Jack.

Ignoring her more logical instincts and giving into her more carnal ones, Annaya leaned forward and pulled Jack towards her. She pressed her lips down over his in an urgent, passionate kiss. Immediately, he responded to her advances and he pushed her down on the sofa, kissing her deeply and hungrily.

Annaya's heart began to beat faster and a flush rose up her face from sexual excitement and her attraction to him. She eagerly pulled his face down to hers to kiss him even more deeply. Her hands ran over the broad length of his strong shoulders and she could feel every firm muscle beneath his shirt.

She was wearing a light pink buttoned blouse and Jack began to pull those buttons open, one at a time, exposing her white lacy bra and the smooth curve of her breasts. One of his hands cupped the lace while his other sunk into her hair and his lips continued to press down over hers, his tongue parting her lips and tasting her.

Her head spun with arousal and the scent of Jack's musky aftershave as he kissed her again. She ripped off his shirt. Beneath the thin material, his body was even more incredible than she'd remembered. He was lean and sculpted and she ran a finger down his washboard stomach. Jack reached around to unhook her bra and let the white lace fall to the ground.

His eyes lit up at the sight of her round breasts freed and he brought his mouth down to suck on one of her dark nipples. Annaya buried her fingers in his smooth hair and bit down on her lip as his tongue flicked over her nipple and made her body tingle and begin to ache with desire. She wanted him desperately.

Jack reached down to unbutton her denim jeans and pulled them from her body, followed by her lacy white panties. When she was completely naked on the sofa, he took a moment to hover above her and drink in the sight.

Her frothy hair fell over her shoulders, her pert breasts heaved as her aroused breaths came fast and heavy and her perfect hourglass figure seemed even more perfect when she reached up to pull him back down to kiss her again.

Jack's hands ran down over her slim navel and then his fingers crept down between her legs. He pushed her thighs apart and his thumb sought out her clitoris. He began to expertly tease her until the pleasure began to make her gasp and grip at the armrest behind her head. He brought her to a powerful orgasm and she cried out loudly. Then Jack pulled off his pants and underpants and while she was still trembling from the orgasm he'd just given her, he thrust deeply into her and made a new wave of pleasure rush over her.

Annaya grasped at his shoulders and moved her hips into his powerful thrusts, gasping and growing breathless as wave after wave of bliss made her grow weak. Finally, Jack gave one final thrust and came inside her. Then he fell down on top of her and kissed her inner neck. Annaya buried her fingers in the hair at the back of his head as the tremors died down and then she felt that sadness return. She wished that Jack didn't have to go.

*****

Jack slept in the guest room that night and Annaya in her own bed. It felt strange to know that he was so close but that they were in separate beds. She wished that they had more of a connection that would make sleeping in the same bed feel more natural, but they both knew that even with a surprise pregnancy, their relationship had still been just about the sex.

Annaya foresaw a lot of heartbreak ahead of her; just because she and Jack had an undeniable and irrepressible chemistry between them that she predicted would see them always blurring the lines between just friends and something more.

Not that she expected a relationship to arise from their bedroom antics, but she could no more imagine them sitting side by side on the sofa as they had done that night and not end up sleeping together.

Of course, the chemistry was there now, but Annaya wondered how she'd feel when her stomach began to swell from the pregnancy and she was waddling around and Jack would undoubtedly gravitate towards the company of other women.

Would she be jealous? Would she be lonely? She didn't want to think about it, so she pulled the covers up over her head, curled up into a ball and thought about the next awkward conversation that they'd undoubtedly be having the next day.

When the morning came, Annaya set about making another coffee and didn't mention the sex they'd had last night, which, like the first night of lovemaking between them, quickly became an event they didn't speak about.

She was relieved when Jack greeted her with a smile and he accepted his coffee without saying anything himself. A silent agreement not to mention the raging sexual attraction between them or what it meant for the future, was made and they both moved onto speaking about other things.

"Will you call me if there's anything you need?" Jack urged her, as he got ready to leave for the airport that day. "You don't have to hesitate to ask."

"I'm fine, Jack. It'll be a while before I need anything. Thank God. I'd have hated to have been huge at

Natalie's wedding. The bridesmaid's dress will still fit."

"I'm sure you'll look beautiful."

Annaya gave him a grateful smile, but sighed. "I was looking forward to it, but now I just can't wait to get through it."

"Why?"

"Because weddings are full of people who've got their lives sorted," Annaya told him. "I could have coped with being on my own, but I'm not sure I can face being single and knocked up. I'm just a disaster."

Jack frowned and caught her by the hand. He caught her eye and said firmly, "You're not a disaster, Annaya. In fact, I think you're being very strong in the face of a difficult situation."

"You're kind, Jack, but wrong. Nothing's gone to plan."

"Would it help if I came with you to the wedding?"

Annaya shot him a look of surprise. "What if someone took a photo? Wouldn't that blow your cover?"

"I think I'd be safe over here. I'll come with you, if you like."

"Do you mean it?"

"Yes. Didn't I say that if I ever saw you again I'd take you on a real date? This will be it. It's the least I can do, considering."

"That would mean a lot. Thank you."

Annaya felt her heart lift at the prospect of having a

date to Natalie's wedding. It was bad enough having to ward off questions about why she was nearly thirty and still single without the secret knowledge that she was also pregnant with an unplanned child.

Plus, it meant that Jack was serious about supporting her. It wasn't a marriage proposal, but it was an offer of more than money. It was a promise to give her moral support and Annaya knew that she'd be in need of that far more than money as the months rolled by.

She was disappointed when it was time for Jack to go. The meeting had been strange, swinging between not knowing what to say to one another and not being able to keep their hands off one another, but with Jack's promise to come with her to Natalie's wedding, Annaya was hopeful that a relationship of more substance could form. Even if she and Jack weren't destined for a great romance, it would be nice to know that they could be friends.

She didn't expect her one-night stand to drop everything to start a relationship with her just because she'd gotten pregnant. But it meant a lot to her to know that she could rely on the father of her child for support when it was needed.

At last, Jack left and Annaya stood at the window for a while after he'd gone, just staring at the spot where his expensive car had been parked. She still wasn't sure how she felt about the man. There was still so much about him that she didn't know. She felt that he was a man that had his priorities all wrong.

She didn't like how he was so concerned with what the public would make of his actions and she wished that the worry of the press wasn't hanging over them.

Annaya would much prefer that her unplanned pregnancy was a private scandal and not at risk of becoming a national one. She also wished that Jack's first concern would be her and not his reputation, but she knew that whatever kind of relationship she ended up having with Jack, that it wouldn't be conventional.

He was a billionaire, after all, which was easy to forget when they were eating Chinese out of foil tins in her cramped apartment, but it was true, all the same. There were eyes on him and he had responsibilities that she could never understand.

His values were different from hers and Annaya could tell that it would be a battle to bring him down from his pedestal and make him see her for who she was – not a PR disaster waiting to happen. She was not an obstacle to his father's fortune, but a human woman, with thoughts and feelings and a baby growing inside her. Annaya finally tore herself away from the window, not sure if she felt any better for having seen Jack. There were still too many things that were uncertain.

Annaya took a deep breath and told herself to calm down. He'd come, hadn't he? He promised he'd take care of her. Annaya knew that Jack would not leave her wanting for the material things, not when there was the risk that one day the world would ask him to answer for his actions. But she worried that would be all he'd offer her. She thought ahead to Natalie's wedding and it cheered her up a little. It wasn't much, but it was a start: a real date with Jack Casali.

Chapter 5

The morning of Natalie's wedding, Annaya was a nervous wreck. She honestly hadn't expected Jack to keep his word and be her date, but she'd just received a call to say that he was on his way to the venue. That made it very hard for Annaya to concentrate on her role as maid of honor.

Her thoughts kept wandering back to her night with Jack at her apartment and the way that they'd ripped each other's clothes off, despite the drama that was unfolding and she wondered what would happen to them on a night where romance was naturally in the air.

Annaya fluffed up the many layers of the skirts on

Natalie's wedding dress with an absent smile, but her thoughts came fully back to the present when she stood back at last and looked at Natalie fully dressed for her wedding day.

She was a beautiful bride. The petite woman was wearing a classic fairy-tale wedding dress, pure white, with a skirt that reached halfway across the room and a veil that fell to the floor. Her black hair had been curled into sweet ringlets and her make-up had given her a fresh-faced bridal look. She looked gorgeous and Annaya felt her eyes fill up with tears.

It felt like the end of an era. She and Natalie had been best friends forever. They'd gotten into mischief together at school and helped each get ready for prom. They'd gone to colleges nearby each other and spent those years out on the town, living life to the fullest. They'd travelled together and been there for one another through thick and thin. Annaya had even been there the night that Natalie met the man that she was marrying that day. Annaya was so happy for Natalie and pleased for her that she'd found somebody who loved her so much, but, at the same time, Annaya felt grieved to be giving away her best friend and left to face the fact that she would be on her own and with a baby on the way.

"Oh Natalie!" she gushed proudly. "You look beautiful."

Natalie was tearful too and swirled in front of the full-length mirror with a happy smile. "I can't believe I'm getting married today."

"He's a lucky man."

Annaya had never been the sort of girl to spend long hours fantasizing over her wedding day and over finding the perfect man. She'd never kept little lists in her notebook of the house she wanted to own and the names of her future children. Natalie had always been the one desperate to settle down and be a wife and mother, while Annaya had always been much more inclined to let her youth last as long as possible and to get the most out of every single moment of being young.

Looking at Natalie now, however, it hit her just how much she *did* want all of those things; marriage, a sweet little house with a picket fence and kids. It also hit her just how royally she'd already screwed up that vision.

It was much more likely that she'd end up in some

budget apartment on her office assistant's wage, juggling part-time work and a baby, as a single mom, desperately putting up profiles on an online dating site, in the hope that she wouldn't be alone forever. She shook her head to shake herself out of her moroseness. This was Natalie's day and not the time for Annaya to feel sorry for herself and regret her own silly decisions.

She and the other bridesmaids finished helping Natalie get ready and then Annaya left the room while the photographer came to take photos of the bride with her parents. Annaya took a moment to creep away behind the church and let a couple of tears fall as she thought about her own future. She jumped when she felt a hand on her shoulder and was shocked when she looked up to see Jack Casali standing there. She quickly wiped her eyes, forced a smile and lifted her gaze to look at him.

He looked incredible in his wedding suit. His dark hair was combed neatly back and he was clean-shaven for the occasion. Looking around at all the other men in their suits and ties, Annaya could honestly say that he was hands-down the most attractive man there and every time she looked at him, she got butterflies.

"Are you alright?"

"I'm fine. It's just... weddings, you know? Natalie looks beautiful."

"So do you."

The bridesmaids were wearing floor-length pink gowns and Annaya's body, in particular, was flattered by the cut. The light material draped over her slim waist and emphasized the curves of her chest in a way that made her look like a Greek goddess. Her frothy hair had been pinned back in places to frame her face and her big, dark eyes had been left natural, apart from a quick lick of mascara that gave her lashes an alluring appearance. She blinked back the last of her tears and lifted herself on her tiptoes to greet Jack with a kiss on the cheek.

"I didn't think you'd come."

"I said I would."

"We should join the others."

Annaya was surprised when Jack held out his hand to her to lead her back towards the crowd. She slipped her hand into his and immediately felt stronger. Jack had such a presence about him, an authority, a *power*,

117

that it made her feel more able to face the world just by being close to him. He'd made her feel like a mistake several times since their night together in Vegas, but him being here meant a lot to her.

"How are you feeling?" Jack asked her. "Is everything going OK with the... you know?"

"The pregnancy? It's still early days yet, Jack. I'm only eight weeks along. The first scan will be at twelve weeks."

"Do you want me to be there?"

Annaya gave him a grateful smile, but shook her head. "You don't have to do that, Jack."

"Do what?"

"Pretend."

"I know all of this has been a surprise, but I'm not a monster, Annaya. I don't expect you to do all those big things on your own. I said I'd support you, and I will."

"Won't people get suspicious if you keep jetting off to California every other week?"

"I'm doing what I can to cover my tracks. I've begun talks to buy some land in California to build a casino. That will explain my presence here."

Annaya felt disappointed again. She didn't like the way he was treating her, like some dirty secret. What did he think would happen when she'd had the baby? Would he hide her behind a big pair of sunglasses and dress her in some oversized poncho to keep her identity hidden?

"What will you tell people when the baby is born?"

"People won't know."

"What about your parents?"

Jack let out a tense sigh. "I'll handle that hurdle when it comes to it."

"I'm sure they'll want to meet their grandchild."

"I suppose you're right. It's just, the way things are... the timing will have to be right before I tell them anything."

"I know the night in Vegas was a mistake, but all of this secrecy seems a bit extreme, Jack. People make mistakes."

They began to file into church with the others and milled around the edges of the pews for a while as they waited for the ceremony to begin. Annaya noticed how the eyes of the other bridesmaids kept drifting over to Jack with interest. His evident wealth and incredible good-looks had become a talking point for the guests and even from their spot slightly removed from the crowds, Annaya could make out snippets of conversation from people trying to guess who he was.

"And you?" Jack said suddenly. "Have you told anyone?"

"My parents know I'm pregnant, but they don't know who the father is."

"I'm sorry for that."

"I hope you change your mind at some point. I imagine they think I'm not telling them who the father

121

is because I don't know myself. It's not nice to have your parents think you've been sleeping around."

"You're right. I'm sorry, Annaya, but I appreciate what you're doing for me. A story like this getting out could ruin me and be bad news for my father, too."

"I think you're blowing it out of proportion. I mean, would anyone really care?"

"The public loves a scandal."

Annaya decided not to press the issue any further. It seemed to make Jack uncomfortable and it made her angry, so she decided to focus instead on the day ahead of them and trying to enjoy it as much as possible despite everything that was happening.

The vicar entered the church and Annaya had to leave Jack to take a seat while she headed to the front of the church to stand in place as Natalie's maid of honor. Thoughts of Jack and the pregnancy faded away as the music began to play and Natalie appeared through the doorways at the end of the aisle. She looked stunning in her dress and seemed to glide down the aisle with her father on her arm. She was absolutely beaming and Annaya was smiling, too. There wasn't a dry eye in the church as she exchanged her vows with John and when the vicar finally announced, "You may now kiss the bride," the crowd erupted into applause.

Everyone was focusing on the bride and groom, yet, when Annaya lifted her eyes to the spectators, she saw that Jack's eyes were focused only on her. She smiled at him and he smiled back and in that short instance, she let herself believe that everything would be alright.

*****

The second Jack had seen her in her pink dress, he'd been hit all over again with that crazy attraction to her. There was just something about Annaya, something he couldn't quite place, which drove him mad. It must have been what the romantics out there called "chemistry" and it seemed a good way to describe it, as Jack felt like he had no control over the way his heart fluttered every time he looked at her.

Jack was not a romantic and he certainly wasn't the soppy, overly-emotional type, but around Annaya, a different side of him seemed to emerge, a side that was protective and tender and it made him do crazy things, like take a flight out to California to be a wedding date for a one-night stand.

He thought back to all the women he'd known in his

time. There had been Tracy when he'd been in his early twenties. She'd probably been the closest thing he'd ever had to a childhood sweetheart. They'd known each other since their school years, when their parents had bonded over their rare car collections. They found themselves thrown together at various upscale events and then ended up in the same high school in their teens.

They'd bumped into each other again when Jack had been twenty-one and they'd dated for a few years. It had been fun at the time, but Jack had soon came to feel bored in the relationship, like he was dating his sister instead of someone that he had a romantic interest in, and it had ended.

Then there had been Hannah when he'd been twenty-five. She'd been a wild card. He'd met her at around that time when Jack had been taking the fullest advantage of his father's credit card and was at his most rebellious. That had ended because their whole relationship had revolved around alcohol and being seen by the press. She'd been trouble and he'd been dating her because he'd like projecting the image of a "bad boy."

After he'd matured a little, he dated a woman named Susan for a while, but their routine soon became too predictable and he was bored again. There was a certain cycle to Jack's relationships. He'd always date a woman for the wrong reasons and then grow bored.

Things felt different with Annaya. He couldn't believe that he'd ever grow bored with her. She was enchanting. Watching the way the future mother of his child's eyes brimmed with tears at the sight of her friend in a wedding dress, made Jack feel guilty that their own relationship had been less than the fairytale romance.

He was aware that his insistence on secrecy was probably not particularly appealing to her, but Jack's experience with women had left him wary of introducing them to the public eye. Hannah, whom he'd dated when he was drinking too much and getting into trouble, had relished the limelight and it had turned her into a clingy, demanding monster and Jack remembered how difficult it had been to break away from her when she'd had the press as her weapon.

It was bad enough breaking up with her when the world was watching, so Jack could only imagine what kind of a difficult position he'd end up in if a pregnant woman began to manipulate the press.

Jack knew all too well that journalists loved nothing more than to vilify a big name and he didn't want to expose himself to their stories. That was why he wanted to keep the pregnancy a secret and protect himself from a journalistic backlash, but he did feel guilty at how his decision was affecting Annaya.

He respected the woman. He wasn't ready for kids himself and a surprise baby certainly hadn't been something he'd anticipated, but he admired how Annaya had stepped up to the mark without a fuss and without any demand for a payout.

That already put her head and shoulders above most of the other women he'd ever been with and that was before he'd even taken into account her beauty and all the other qualities he was sure he had left to discover.

When the ceremony finished, Jack stood at a distance as Annaya was pulled away to take photographs as part of the bridal party. She was easily the most beautiful woman in the group and he could hardly tear his eyes away from her and her dazzling smile. She was simply stunning.

Finally, the photos had all been taken and Annaya returned to him. He held out his arm to her and they began to walk to the waiting cars to head to the reception, which was being held at a luxurious hotel.

"It was a beautiful ceremony," Jack said.

"It was, wasn't it?"

"Did you ever want to get married?"

"You make it sound like that option's closed off to me now."

"I didn't mean it like that."

"Yes, I did want to get married. I guess I just always thought I had all the time in the world to meet 'the one' and settle down. The timeline's been thrown off a bit now, though. I hope you're not mad at me for keeping it."

"Of course not. It's your decision."

"Did you plan on having kids?"

"I don't know. One day, maybe. Like you, I thought I had all the time in the world to think of things like that. Right now, I guess I'd say I don't really consider myself father material."

"No? Why not?"

"It's a lot of responsibility taking care of a kid."

"You think you wouldn't be able to step up? Well, if it's any consolation, you've done alright stepping up so far and for what it's worth, I'm glad you're here."

No, being a father was not something that had ever really crossed Jack's mind. He'd been far too preoccupied with living the high life and trying to live up to his father's expectations. The thought of a little Jack Casali running around was one that made him worry – any kid of his would be a little hell raiser!

He looked over at Annaya and smiled with amusement. She was just the same, a little wild. Yes, they certainly had their work cut out for them. He slipped his hand into hers and gave it a squeeze and she shot him one of her grateful little glances and a relieved smile.

He couldn't believe that it was only eight weeks ago

that they'd first met and that it had all begun with a drunken night gone too far. Now, the shape of his whole world had changed and whatever happened, he and Annaya were bound together now by the life that was growing inside of her. Yet, whenever he looked at that beautiful smile and her big, dark eyes, the thought didn't seem quite so bad.

*****

Jack and Annaya sat next to each other at the reception when they were dining and it meant that they were finally able to speak properly. It was strange that the awkwardness between them still prevailed after everything, but Annaya was desperate to get to know him and be done with the formality. She was having his baby. God knew she was going to know something about the father.

"Tell me about you, Jack. Even after everything, I feel like we're still strangers."

"What do you want to know?"

"Surprise me."

"Alright. Well, I was born and raised in Vegas, but I studied business at Harvard."

Annaya laughed out loud and then laid an apologetic hand on his arm. "I'm sorry. I didn't mean to laugh. I just can't imagine you at Harvard. You don't seem the type."

"I know, I know," Jack chuckled, "but I suppose I'm actually rather academic. I must have got that from my father. I didn't want to go to college, but he insisted. I did very well, got my degree and then went back to doing what I do best – enjoying life. What about you?"

"Did I study? Yes, I did. I studied Business, too."

"You're joking?"

"No, I really did. I wanted to start my own internet company, but I had to get a job to pay my way and then I just never really got around to making it happen."

"What kind of business would it have been?"

"Business consultancy."

"Wow. So you're smart."

"Just not as ditzy as I seem. Like you, I let my spontaneity take over sometimes."

They smiled at each other. It was something of a

revelation to each learn that the other was educated. The way that they had met made each naturally assume that the other was too wild to have ever spent long nights in the library, but they were finding that they both had a lot to learn about each other and more in common than either had realized.

"It must have been strange growing up in such a wealthy family," Annaya commented. "I can't imagine having everything I ever wanted."

"It had its perks," Jack admitted, "but when you're born into a successful family there's a lot of expectations on you. And you? What is your family like?"

"Normal," Annaya laughed. "My mother is a nurse. My father is a car salesman. I have a younger sister. She's married with two kids."

"That must be tough."

"Why? Because all women are meant to be married with kids by twenty-five?"

"That's what all the women I've dated have made it seem like."

"Have you ever been tempted to propose to any of them?"

Jack pulled a face. "I can't imagine being with one woman for the rest of my life. All the women I've dated have changed over time into people I don't like or worse, stayed exactly the same and then I get bored."

"So you need a woman that surprises you?"

"That's right. A smart, sexy woman who's not afraid

of a few surprises herself."

Annaya realized that she'd begun to lean in closer to him and that she was running her finger around the rim of her glass of water in a way that could be described as suggestive. She quickly drew back from him with an embarrassed smile. She couldn't explain the effect that Jack Casali had on her. Somehow he just made her into this little minx.

Granted, she was known as a bit of a flirt and when she saw a man she was attracted to, Annaya had never been afraid to make the first move, but with Jack it was more than that. He made her so very aware that she was a woman and he was a man and all she wanted to do every time she looked at him was sink into another one of his kisses. She wondered how damaging that magnetism would be when a kid was involved and they had more important things to think about than her place or his.

"There'll be far fewer surprises soon," she said quickly, getting what was on her mind out of her mouth and turning away from him to distract herself from the smooth gaze of his eyes.

"What do you mean?"

"Well, once there's a kid, life finds a routine, doesn't it? It'll start off with nap schedules and feeding times and then it'll turn into the school run and a homework timetable. It will be eighteen years of predictable."

Jack smiled at her in a way that was almost fond. "I can't imagine that you'll ever be predictable."

"I'll be a mom."

"I'll be a dad."

Annaya let out a light little laugh. "Well, I know that you'll never be predictable."

"There you go. Things will just be a little different."

"Do you think you'll be there in his or her life? Our son's or daughter's?"

"I hope to be. I hardly ever saw my dad growing up. I was always with a member of staff. He was always at work. I always told myself that if I ever had kids, I'd be involved in their life."

"The distance will make it difficult."

"We'll figure it out. You could come to Vegas."

"Vegas?" Annaya let out a little laugh. "I don't want to raise a kid in Vegas. He'll grow up to be a gambler who hangs out in strip clubs."

Jack laughed at her assumption and raised his eyebrows in amusement. "Now, I didn't turn out so bad, did I?"

Annaya realized her stereotypes covered him and she laughed herself. "No. I suppose not."

*****

The first dance was a magical moment between bride and groom. Natalie's eyes were shining with love for her new husband and Daniel was looking down at her with beg, tender eyes and his arms about her waist.

A love song came on and they began to sway in the middle of the dance floor as everyone let out little "awws." Annaya watched them with a little twinge of sadness and tried not to look too upset when all of the other couples began to get up and join them on the dance floor.

Suddenly, Jack stood up from his chair and held out his hand to her. "Will you dance with me?"

Annaya was left momentarily speechless by how sweet she found his gesture. After all, who was she to him except for some woman he'd slept with a couple of times and made his life more difficult? Yet, here he was, reaching out to her and making sure she didn't feel alone on a night meant for lovers. She took hold of his hand and followed him in a kind of trance to the dance floor.

Once there, he threaded his arm around her waist and pulled her close to him. Annaya felt that attraction to him coursing through her veins once again and she was left breathless by how amazing it felt to be in his arms, moving in little circles to the sound of a sweet melody.

She began by dancing with a little space between them, but as the music played on, she let her head rest against his chest and he didn't step back. Rather, he rested his chin against her head and they swayed together closely. It was a bittersweet moment.

It meant the world to Annaya that he'd stopped her being alone tonight and was having a moment of closeness with her like this, but it also broke her heart that in the morning he'd be flying back out to Vegas and all the reality of what was really happening would come crashing back down onto her shoulders. She had to tell herself that this wasn't romance. This was just the calm before the storm.

*****

Dancing with Annaya brought back all those calm and tender feelings that Jack had never felt before. Annaya had such grace and when she laid her head against his chest, it had made Jack feel such a surge of affection; something different from lust or sexual desire, something much sweeter. It made him slightly morose to think of what could have been in different circumstances, but unfortunately his status would not allow him to welcome a one-night stand into his life. His father would go berserk if he were to introduce her to him under these circumstances and she lived in California and wanted to stay there for the baby.

Besides, Jack had to tell himself, that *the way he felt around Annaya was not a growing love or anything special, it was just the way any man would feel to be close to someone carrying his child. It was an appreciation for a beautiful woman.*

The wedding would have been a joyous affair if Jack and Annaya hadn't both had other things on their mind, but they had moments of laughter amongst the worry. It had been nice to talk to Annaya over dinner and learn a little more about her upbringing and family and the dance they'd shared had been a few minutes of solace that Jack was sure he'd never forget. Now the night was over and they were left with the same decision that they'd been left with before. Take it to the bedroom, or walk away.

"I'm staying in the hotel tonight," Jack informed her, as they stood in the lobby of the grand reception as the guests filed out. He looked meaningfully up towards the spiral staircase leading up towards the room. "Would you like to talk a little longer?"

"Alright."

Jack knew the second she agreed that they would doubtlessly find themselves in each other's arms again and he wasn't sure how he felt about it. Annaya was beautiful, her body was incredible and that one night they'd made love when they hadn't both been drunk out of their minds had been unforgettable, but he was worrying that this would turn into a habit that would create problems down the line. Yet, even though he knew there were reasons to be cautious, he couldn't stop himself from taking hold of Annaya's hand and leading her into his room.

Once they were in the hotel suite, his jacket came off immediately and he pressed his lips down over hers. At first, Annaya returned his kiss eagerly, but then he felt her hands pressing against his chest to push him away and she stepped back with slightly tearful eyes and brushed back her hair from her face with a weary hand.

"I'm sorry, Jack. I shouldn't have come up here. This was a mistake."

"No, don't be sorry," Jack conceded, respectfully taking a step away from her and sitting slightly dejected on the edge of his bed. "You're right. This would be a mistake."

Tentatively, Annaya came to sit at his side on the bed and she bit down on her lip nervously, shooting him sideways glances and her fingers fiddled with the seams on the bedcovers. Eventually she sighed and tried to explain herself.

"We're going to be in each other's lives from now on and I don't know how that's going to turn out. I don't know if I'm going to see you once a month or once a year. I don't know if we'll end up really good friends or hardly more than we are now. The one thing I do know is that I'm not looking for someone to screw every time he's in town, only to be on my own again as soon as he takes off the next day. I need more security in my life than that."

Jack put a hand on her shoulder reassuringly. "You don't have to explain yourself to me. You're right. There's chemistry between us, for sure, but we can't let it take over. There's too much at stake for that."

"Are you thinking of the press again?" Annaya asked, with a slightly judging tone to her voice.

Jack half-laughed at her cynicism and shook his head. "More than that, Annaya. We're going to have a kid."

He fell back onto the bed and stared up at the ceiling

as though the sudden realization had overwhelmed him. Annaya followed suit and also fell onto her back at his side to stare up at the white plaster and let reality sink in.

"We're going to have a kid," she repeated.

There was a moment's silence between them as all that chemistry which had been fizzing between them came to a standstill and they lay side by side as the future mother and father of their unborn child. Then Jack turned his head towards her and smiled. She smiled back and slipped her hand into his and they lay for while just like that, side by side and saying nothing, as if waiting for an easy answer, which never came.

Chapter6

Back in Vegas, Jack couldn't keep his mind on work, on his social life, or on anything else. Night and day, all that was on his mind was Annaya. He felt terrible to be so far from her, although he made an effort to call her at least once a week and check up on her and the baby. She said she was doing fine and Jack was sure that everything was progressing alright with the pregnancy, but he worried far more about how she was coping on her own.

"You've been moping around for weeks, Jack," Lewis confronted him when they were having dinner one night in a members-only club. "What is going on?"

Jack looked around the expensive bar furtively and leaned in closer to Lewis. "Can you keep something to yourself?"

"Is it to do with that woman from the casino?"

"How did you guess?"

"You've been different ever since you've met her. I had a feeling you were still in touch with her. What is it? Has she threatened to go to the press with it? Is she blackmailing you? Demanding money?"

"No! Nothing like that."

"Then what is it?"

"She's pregnant."

"Pregnant? Jack, are you sure? I don't mean to be a cynic, but any girl's got a lot to gain from pretending to be carrying your child."

"She's not like that."

"How could you know? You barely know the woman."

"Trust me, Lewis. She's not after anything."

"Well, I hope you're right. Jesus, Jack. That's a bit of a problem. What are you going to do?"

"I'm still trying to figure it out."

"Is she going to keep it?"

"Yes."

"Wow. I bet your father's going to have something to say about that. I suppose you haven't told him?"

"Of course I haven't."

"He'll find out eventually, one way or another."

"I know."

"And you trust this girl to keep quiet?"

"I told you, Lewis. I trust her."

Lewis sat back in his chair and gave a casual shrug. "Then it's up to you to make the next move, Jack. You're going to have to come clean to your father and you'll probably have to arrange a public announcement for the press."

"I don't want the press getting hold of this."

"You know they will."

"I don't want to drag Annaya into all of that. It's bad enough that I've got her pregnant and she's a plane ride away. I can't stop thinking about how she's on her own over in California and how she's promised to keep her mouth shut. She won't even tell her parents that I'm the father."

"It's probably for the best until you've figured out how you're going to frame it."

"How can I frame it, Lewis? It is what it is. I drank too much and got a girl pregnant."

"You'll have to spin it differently for the press. Pretend that it's the culmination of a long-term love affair."

"Hmph."

"I don't know what to tell you, Jack. You'll have to face it sometime. People are going to find out."

Jack knew Lewis was right, but the thought of telling his father that he'd done something reckless again made Jack feel like a child and he'd much rather tell him at a time when he'd figured a few things out and could frame it in a better light.

After dinner, he said goodbye to Lewis and began to head out of the club. He was just walking towards the valet to hand over his keys when suddenly he heard his name being called and turned around to find a familiar woman waving at him.

It was Hannah. She was as beautiful as ever, but it had been a while since Jack had seen her in the cold light of day. The slim blonde was wearing a soft pink cashmere sweater and a short black skirt. She looked every bit the Stepford wife, but Jack knew better than to be deceived by appearances. He knew with just a few shots in her, Hannah would be dancing on the tables and telling the press all her dirty secrets. Jack let out a little groan when he realized who was calling him and impatiently waited for her to catch up. She greeted him by throwing her arms around his neck with a little squeal.

"Jack! Darling! It's been too long! Where have you been?"

"Oh, you know, around."

"I've been trying to get a hold of you for weeks. In fact, I was telling Sophie just the other day about how I needed to have a good old catch up with Jack. When are you free, darling? We should get some drinks."

"I'm not really into all that anymore, Hannah."

"Nonsense! We used to have such fun! Do you remember?"

Jack pulled a face. The last night out he'd had with Hannah had ended in disaster when one of the young men they'd been driving with had been pulled over for drunk driving and the papers had broadcast the dangerous activities of Vegas' young and wealthy. His father had been furious at him for having been involved in the scandal. Things had only been made worse by Hannah's eagerness to provide a quote for the paper and all because she loved being at the center of attention of a group of journalists.

It was her big mouth that had tied Jack's name to the incident and he'd made an effort to stay away from both her and the others since that night in an effort to clear up his act and prove to his father that he was worthy of inheriting the family business.

"Don't be a bore, Jack. Let's meet up sometime."

"Really, Hannah, I don't think it's a good idea. I'm working towards taking over the casinos. I really need to focus on my work right now."

Hannah's eyes lit up at the mention of his inheritance and she moved her body closer to him suggestively. "What a big responsibility that must be. I'd love to hear all about it sometime. I'll call you."

A valet appeared at that moment with Hannah's car and the manipulative blonde drove away. Jack rolled his eyes. He knew just why Hannah was so interested in talking to him again. It had been all over the business reports that her father's own company had suffered a monumental loss in recent months after a huge contract fell through and that her family's funds were in danger.

She was looking to latch onto a wealthy partner to

keep her in the lifestyle to which she was accustomed and, as a former flame, Jack was naturally her first choice. In his younger days, Jack might have fallen for her charms, but he'd had enough women attaching themselves to him for his bank account; by now that he'd learned to sense a gold-digger and Hannah was more than that. She was a gold-digger *and* an attention seeker – a lethal mix to a young billionaire in the public eye. Hannah was one thing: trouble.

*****

It seemed crazy to Annaya that she could miss Jack after having spent so little time with him, but she certainly missed the way he made her feel. As she went about her daily life in his absence, her thoughts kept drifting back to that dance they'd shared. For some reason, that moment of sweet intimacy between them stuck out in her mind far more than the night they'd made love.

She'd felt safe with him then, and special, like a princess when everyone saw her in the arms of the most handsome man in the world. Every time that she looked at Jack, Annaya felt her heart lift and without him around, nothing else seemed quite as exciting. She looked forward with great anticipation to Friday nights when he would call her and ask her how she was doing and if everything was alright with the baby.

At first, the calls had been short and formal, with him simply asking whether there was anything she needed and asking for reminders for the next important date in the pregnancy. But as the weeks passed, the phone calls became friendlier, and Annaya began to ask how *he* was.

At first, he'd chuckled at her attempts to engage him in chit-chat, but slowly, he began to call prepared for her onslaught of questions and enjoyed the chance to offload on somebody who seemed to enjoy listening to him talk about his work and what he'd been up to with Lewis.

Annaya could feel him relaxing during their conversations and started to feel like they were really getting to know each other, which made her glad, because her worst fear was that he'd leave her alone to raise their child at a time when everyone around her already had enough on their plates with starting their own lives.

It was a little easier when one day, Annaya had Natalie over for coffee and her best friend had some great news.

"Daniel and I have been trying since the wedding, and I'm pregnant!"

"Really?" Annaya gasped. "Natalie, that's *fantastic* news!"

Annaya threw her arms around her friend and felt a huge wave of relief well up within her. Natalie wasn't a boyfriend or husband, but she would be someone who knew what she was going through and Annaya found her advice invaluable in the weeks that followed.

Where Annaya had kind of just let the pregnancy go along in its own manner, Natalie was forever reading books and doing internet research on how to keep the baby healthy and what kinds of diet to eat. Natalie knew week by week how big the baby would be by hen and at what stage the baby would develop fingers and toes or a smile.

Annaya was glad to have someone around her who knew what she was doing, but she always felt that familiar pang of longing whenever Daniel joined in the conversation.Annaya wished that she had a partner with her too. It was great to talk to Jack on the phone, but really, she longed for him to be with her in person, on-call when she needed him.

She knew that he was just on the other end of the line, but she didn't quite feel like they were close enough yet for her to feel it was OK to just call him out-of-the-blue. They had their Friday night chats and she had to be content with that.

The next time she saw him in person was four weeks

after Natalie's wedding, for the first scan. She went to pick him up at the airport, after insisting that he didn't have to waste money on a company car when she was able to drive him. He'd laughed at that, reminding her that money was not really an issue, but Annaya had told him that their child was going to learn the value of money and that budgeting was an important part of real life.

"Real life, huh?" Jack had laughed. "What does that make this?"

"It still feels like a dream to me."

The third time Annaya had seen Jack on her home ground in Bakersfield felt different to the two times before, due to the conversations they'd had on the phone and the feeling that they knew each other just a little better now.

Jack rested his hand on the back of her headrest as she drove and Annaya felt her heart beating faster, once again having his body so close to hers. It felt strange to have him in her car, like a fantasy had come to life and entered the real world.

Even now, Annaya couldn't help but put Jack on a pedestal. He was just incredible in every way: handsome, intelligent, and wealthy. It made it hard for any hot-blooded woman to keep her cool in his presence, but she and Jack had discussed the fact that they needed to find a way to keep their hands off each other as the pregnancy progressed.

They were going to be parents soon and had to stop acting like horny teens if there was no chance it would turn into something more serious. That seemed unlikely as long as Jack was putting his father's reputation before any romantic potential between them.

Annaya pulled up at the hospital and took a moment to breathe before stepping out of the car. She was a mess of nerves, knowing that as soon as she saw the shadow on the ultrasound screen that all of this would become even more real.

"Are you alright?" Jack asked her.

"We're about to see our baby."

Jack smiled. "It's pretty amazing, isn't it?"

"You think? Are you excited for the baby, Jack?"

The billionaire paused for a moment to consider her question and then a little smile crept onto his face and he nodded. "You know, I actually am. I didn't expect to be, but now that it's happened, I think I'd enjoy having a son or a daughter. Someone to follow in my footsteps."

Annaya laughed. "Hopefully our child will have more sense than us."

"We're not so bad."

The two smiled at each other and Jack stepped out of the car. He came around to the driver's side, pulled the door open and held out a hand to Annaya to encourage her to step out. "Come on, Annie. It's going to be alright."

Annaya's heart gave another little flutter when he called her "Annie." Nobody had ever shortened her name before or had a nickname for her, but she loved that Jack had said it. It made her feel like they were closer than they realized. It felt special that he called her something that nobody else did, even if it was just '"Annie" and not "darling" or "sweetheart" or any other term of endearment that most mothers would expect from the fathers of their children.

She took his hand. It was amazing how every time she took his hand, she felt like she was taking hold of a lifeline, like he was anchoring her and making her feel safe. She wished that she could hold onto his hand forever. She stepped out of the car and Jack put his arm around her as they headed towards the hospital.

Once inside, she headed to the maternity ward and to the room where the ultrasound would take place. It was a small, clinical room with a waxy examination table in the middle of the room, a lime green curtain on a rail and the ultrasound machine in the corner.

Annaya was instructed to lie on the examination table

and lift up the bed. She did as she was told and self-

consciously ran her hand over her stomach as the

redheaded nurse began to apply a cool gel to the

scanner. Annaya wasn't showing yet and her stomach

was as smooth and flat as the night she and Jack had

first met.

Annaya gasped when the nurse placed the scanner

down on her skin and the cold gel made her tense.

Jack immediately took a step closer to the bed and

took hold of her hand. She smiled up at him

gratefully, as the nurse began to run the scanner over

her stomach and a grainy little black and white

picture appeared on the tiny ultrasound screen.

"Oh my God," Annaya whispered. "Is that our baby?"

The nurse smiled warmly at them both. "That's your baby. The heartbeat is healthy. Everything looks normal. Would you like a picture?"

"Please."

The nurse hit a button on the machine and a little photo of their tiny unborn baby was printed. She handed the photo to Annaya and she and Jack leaned close together to look at the little picture.

"That's incredible," Jack breathed.

"I know."

Annaya turned to look at him and realized that his face was incredible close to hers, his lips half-an-inch from hers. She desperately wanted to kiss him in the excitement of the moment and in celebration of their beautiful little baby growing healthily, but she didn't want to break the agreement that they'd made to keep their relationship platonic.

It just didn't make sense to start a romance under such difficult circumstances. They hardly knew each other, after all, and they both knew that if they tried to act like a couple for the sake of the baby, then they'd probably end up resenting each other and ruining what could be a peaceful, if somewhat unconventional, family life. Jack locked eyes with her and she could see the same desire lingering there. She quickly turned away and slipped the photo back into her purse. The gel was cleaned off of her stomach and within twenty minutes, the first scan was done.

"My flight doesn't leave again until eight," Jack told her. "Do you want to grab a late lunch somewhere?"

"Sure."

She took him to a quiet little bistro down a backstreet in her hometown. She loved it because it was a little off the beaten track and although it was a little shabby and unknown, the food was great and it felt like a wonderful little secret amongst all the chain restaurants and big brand names.

"It's nice here," Jack commented, when they took their seat inside by the windows.

They were able to look outside from their little perch in the quiet booth and watch the world go by on the street outside. It was a peaceful feeling to be inside and warm on a cold night when others were huddled up in their coats outside.

"This is where I was taken on my first date," she revealed to him. "It was a terrible night. Everything that could have gone wrong, did go wrong. His car wouldn't start and so he was an hour late picking me up, by which time we'd missed our reservation at the first restaurant he'd chosen. We ended up wandering around in the cold until we found this place and then suddenly, everything turned around and we had the most wonderful evening. It didn't last, of course – we were seventeen – but I've always had fond memories of this place. The night could've been such disaster. Nothing went to plan. But it actually ended up being one of the best first dates I've ever had."

"Life works like that sometimes," Jack said wisely. "Things don't go to plan, but it all works out in the end. I can't say that the first date I ever took a girl on went so smoothly."

"What happened?"

"Everything went precisely to plan. I took her to a

nice restaurant. I bought her flowers. I paid for expensive champagne. The whole nine yards."

"And?"

"And she said I was dull!" Jack let out a little laugh and shook his head in amused self-awareness. "She was right, of course. I thought I was doing everything right, doing what the movies had taught me to do, but I don't think I asked her about herself once. I learned a lot from that date."

"So you were pretty arrogant when you were young?"

"I was. It shames me to say it now. I bet you were an angel, weren't you?"

"No way!" Annaya giggled. "I was a tomboy until I was fourteen. I was always climbing trees and catching frogs and driving my mom mad tracking dirt in through the house."

"You? A tomboy?" Jack said with surprise. "I can't imagine that. You're the most beautiful woman I've ever met."

Annaya laughed lightly at his compliment and briefly thought to herself that he was crossing their line by saying that she was beautiful, but then carried on telling him about her childhood. "No, it's true. I was all dungarees and I used to wear my hair up in pigtails with a baseball cap. I used to follow the boys around everywhere and try to get them to let me join in their sports games.

 I only started dressing and acting like a girl when I was fifteen and had my first crush on a boy named Peter Smith. He was mad about pool, so I used to hang around at the pool hall and pretend I knew what

I was doing. I'd lean across the table with my cue and try to catch his eye."

"Ah, so that's where you learned that trick."

Annaya laughed again. "I was a tomboy for all those years, but as soon as I started acting like a girl, it turned out I was a natural flirt. It was like the ugly duckling story. Overnight, boys started looking at me. And my mother was able to finally stop nagging me about wearing denim jeans."

Jack smiled. "I've been thinking about that," he confessed.

"About what?"

"About your parents."

"Go on."

"What I'm asking you isn't fair. I think you should tell them I'm the father. I'll meet them and reassure them that I'm going to do right by you and the baby."

Annaya's face lit up. "Do you mean it?"

"I do. I should never have asked you to keep it from them. I guess that's because I'm not close to my parents, I thought it wouldn't be a big deal to ask you to keep it quiet, but you're not like my family. Go ahead and tell them. I'll be happy to speak to them."

"That means a lot to me, Jack. Thank you."

She beamed at him from across the table and he smiled back. Annaya felt herself feeling finally reassured that Jack was going to offer her more than money. She wanted him to be a part of hers and her child's life and that began with him meeting her parents and accepting his role as part of her family.

She couldn't wait to introduce him to her parents and reassure them that he was going to take care of her. More and more she believed that he would. Breaking their rules again, Annaya reached out her hand across the table and let it rest on the tablecloth facing upwards and slightly open. A happy smile crept onto her face when Jack's hand came to meet it and he closed his fingers around hers.

At the end of the night, Jack seemed reluctant to leave. "It's been good to spend some real time with you tonight, Annaya. I keep forgetting how much there is to learn about you. Our son or daughter is going to be a lucky kid to have a mom like you."

"You're sweet," Annaya smiled. They were at the airport now and waiting in the Departures lounge, looking up at the boards. Annaya felt sad that he was leaving, but that feeling was no longer unfamiliar to her. She knew she'd miss him and how safe he made her feel the second that he stepped on that plane and she'd be back to waiting by the phone, hoping that he'd call off-schedule. The letters on the departure board flipped over and let them know that the flight to Vegas was boarding. Jack looked up at it and sighed heavily.

"I guess that's me. Goodbye, Annaya. Let me know if there's anything you need."

"I will."

Jack gave her a kiss on the cheek in farewell and his lips brushed her skin a moment longer than necessary. The feeling of his stubble on her cheek sent happy shivers down Annaya's spine and she had to draw back to stop herself from throwing her arms around his neck or pressing her lips down over his. "I'll speak to you on Friday."

"Great."

Jack turned to leave when suddenly Annaya remembered something and she called him to a stop. "Wait! I want you to keep this." Annaya reached into her purse and pulled out the ultrasound photo, which she pressed into his hands with a smile. "So you don't forget us when you're in Vegas."

*****

Jack sat in the club with that photo in his hands. He was feeling that strange feeling again that he felt for a few days whenever he left Annaya. Away from her, he missed her big, bright smile, those beautiful eyes and the way her face lit up whenever he offered her his hand.

He couldn't remember the last time a woman had looked at him with affection rather than greed. He liked the way it felt to have a beautiful woman enjoy his company. Nobody else in his life could capture his attention quite the same way.

Since meeting Annaya, Jack had stopped chasing women for the first time since he'd hit puberty. He lost interest since he'd been spending time with the most beautiful woman in the world. Nobody else compared and with the secret of the baby binding them closer, Jack couldn't even consider flirting with anybody else. Not that it stopped certain women from trying.

Hannah was in the private club again. Jack suspected

she'd taken to hanging around there ever since she'd last seen him, in the hopes of seeing him again. He pulled a face when he heard her screech echoing from behind him. He went to place the ultrasound back in his jacket pocket, but Hannah's prying hands pulled it from his grasp before he had a chance.

"What is this?" she asked brightly. Jack spun in his chair to look up at the woman who had appeared from nowhere and sprung across the members' lounge seemingly in a split second to claw that picture from his hands. He calmly stood up and tried to take it back.

"That's private, Hannah."

The blonde's eyes had grown wide with surprise and her mouth fell open slightly. She'd put down the tennis racquet she'd been holding so that she could

move the picture closer to her face and stare
incredulously at the unmistakable outline of a baby.

"Is this a baby scan? Jack! Whose baby is it?"

"Nobody's." Jack quickly reached out and took the
photo from her, placing it back in his pocket. "It's not
for you to worry about."

"Is that yours? Jack, are you having a baby?"

"It's none of your concern, Hannah."

"Does your father know about it?"

"No. And he's not to know, either."

"This seems like some pretty big news, Jack. I'd love
to hear about it over dinner."

Jack glared at her and grit his teeth. Hannah didn't

have to tell him that she was blackmailing him for him to recognize that serpentine smile. "I'm not interested. Thanks."

Hannah sat on the arm of the leather armchair to which Jack had returned and playfully ran a finger down his arm. "We were good together, Jack. We had a lot of fun."

"We were drunk kids who took it too far."

"You were different then. You were fun."

"People change."

"Don't you remember the chemistry between us back then?"

Jack scoffed at that comment before he could stop himself. He couldn't help it. Memories of grinding against Hannah seemed so dull and distant in comparison to the fireworks he'd felt with Annaya that were still fresh in his mind. Even now, the recollection of Annaya's naked body on that sofa made his blood rush. He shot Hannah a scathing glare. "Enough, Hannah. We're not getting back together."

"Why? Because you've knocked someone up? Who is she, Jack? You know, I'm going to get to the bottom of it one way or another."

"Grow up. Just because your Daddy always gave you everything you wanted, doesn't mean you control the rest of us. Try your luck with another member. There are plenty of loaded guys here."

Hannah's face flushed red at his insinuation and she stood up in a huff, her short tennis skirt twirling. She turned on her heel to point a threatening finger in his direction as she left, "I *will* find out who she is."

*

"Annaya, has Jack called?"

Annaya was surprised to get a call from Natalie at 8 am on a Saturday morning and immediately she was concerned. "No, why?"

"He's all over the Vegas news."

"*What?* Is he OK?"

Strangely enough, Annaya's first instinct wasn't that their secret had been discovered, but rather that something bad had happened to Jack and she immediately felt her heart catch in her throat from fear. She didn't know what she'd do if anything happened to him. She missed him like crazy when he was simply out-of-state. The thought of him having been killed was more than she could bear.

"He's alright. Nobody's been hurt."

"Thank God! What is it then?"

"Someone got hold of what happened. I'm reading this trashy Vegas celeb mag. Some *Who's Who* type thing. He's on the front cover. It says *Jack Casali: Soon to be a father?*"

"What? Where did you get that from?"

"I took an interest after you told me you were pregnant. I thought I'd better keep an eye on this guy."

Annaya didn't know whether to laugh or cry. She'd

wished she'd heard it from Jack, but it didn't surprise her that Natalie was the first to know. Her organized friend had always been on top of things and it didn't surprise Annaya at all that she'd been keeping tabs on Jack.

"What does the article say?"

"It says that an anonymous source has suggested that Jack Casali is expecting his first child."

"Oh my God. Does it mention my name?"

"No. It says that the identity of the mother is still a mystery. *Does this mean that the playboy's wild days are finally at an end?*"

"It says that? Oh God, that's so cheesy."

"I know. Vegas reckons that you'll be the one to tie

him down."

"I can't believe it's in a magazine. Who's reading this stuff?"

"A lot of people, apparently. It's on the web, too."

"Are you serious?"

"Look it up."

Annaya typed *Jack Casali* into her search engine and her mouth dropped open as she saw dozens of hits speculating about the billionaire playboy and the identity of his mystery woman. Annaya felt a panic drape over her. What did this mean for her and Jack? Would he deny it and stop seeing her? What would his father say? She bit down on her lips and sunk down onto her sofa.

"What happens now?"

"I don't know. Maybe he'll call. I just thought I'd give you a head's up. Are you alright?"

"I'm fine. Just... shocked."

"You know where I am if you need me."

"Thanks."

Annaya put the phone down and almost immediately it started ringing again. She picked it up quickly and felt a wave of relief followed by a second wave of panic rush over her when she heard Jack's voice down the line.

"Natalie just called. She told me about that magazine. What the hell is going on, Jack? Are we alright?"

"It's a lot to go into, Annie. Long story short, it would

really help me out if you could come over here. Are you free tonight?"

"You want me to come to Vegas?"

"I'll arrange the tickets and somebody to pick you up. My father wants to meet you."

"He knows?"

"Of course he knows. His PR team is having a field day over it. He wants to have an emergency briefing on how to handle it."

"Won't it all just blow over in a couple of days? Does anyone really care about this stuff?"

"More than you'd know. Please, Annie. I need you here."

"Alright. I can come."

*****

It felt more than surreal to step into the First Class section of a plane on her way to see Jack. Annaya's head hadn't stopped spinning since that morning. The whole thing seemed so bizarre to her and she simply couldn't believe anyone cared that much about who Jack Casali had slept with, but then she thought of all those celebrities in the world who were famous for being famous or famous for being rich. She supposed that Jack wasn't so different from any of them. He was insanely wealthy and insanely attractive -- wasn't that enough to make the world take notice?

Not to mention the scores of Vegas women who'd been hoping to be the one to tie the playboy down. It was always news when a rich and eligible bachelor was taken. It was a sad day for the elite when that happened.

The flight went smoothly and by the time that Annaya had collected her case from the carousel and headed into the arrivals lounge, there was already somebody waiting for her with a sign. She headed towards the chauffeur and was taken to a very expensive car.

Annaya felt the panic growing greater and greater within her as they travelled through Vegas towards some unknown destination. She wasn't just meeting with Jack today, but also with his father and she imagined that he'd have something to say about her causing a scandal. She wondered if he'd try to pay her off to keep quiet or send her abroad to live in some distant villa where nobody would ever find her. The way Jack described him, she was expecting his father to go to some kind of extreme length to hush this up.

At last, the car pulled up at a set of tall, ornate black gates, which drifted open as if by magic when the car drew near. The driver drove them up a long, expansive driveway towards a mansion, which lay in the distance. Annaya's eyes grew wider and wider as they drove closer and her gaze travelled over the immaculate estate, its perfect roses, marble steps and the incredible statue which topped the glorious fountain in front of the mansion. It was a palace.

When the car came to a stop in front of the building, a different servant came to open the door and lead her towards the mansion and it was a butler who answered the bell. Annaya had now been in the estate for a good ten minutes and was yet to see anybody who was not a member of staff. She was intimidated by the lack of ordinary people in this place and by the tall ceilings and chandeliers. Everything seemed to be made out of marble or crystal and every surface was topped with some priceless antique.

The lobby looked like it had jumped straight out of some James Bond movie, when the spy meets the billionaire villain on his home ground. As you entered the door, you were met with the sight of a huge sweeping staircase carpeted in a deep red carpet that was meant for wealthy feet.

No matter which way Annaya turned her head, she felt in awe and she felt suddenly very self-conscious to be standing there in a pair of denim jeans and a slightly tatty old purple sweater when she was surrounded by servants in immaculate suits and chandeliers. The butler told her that she'd be met shortly and left her in the lobby. Annaya felt like a deer in headlights waiting for someone to meet her.

She was hoping that Jack would find her soon, before the pressure got too much. Annaya was sure that she was going to faint soon. This whole thing felt like a dream.

She was made even more nervous when she found that it was not Jack who came to greet her in the lobby, but some robust and stern-looking gentleman in an expensive pinstripe suit who looked a lot like Jack. Annaya knew at once that this was Jack's father and she felt herself begin to tremble as he stepped closer. Brandon Casali's face wore an expression of perpetual disappointment and he walked with his hands clasped together behind his back, pursing his lips together critically as he looked her over. Annaya felt terrified to be held there under his glare, but she kept her head held high and tried not to look too unnerved.

She was surprised when the old man's face suddenly broke out into a smile and he reached out to shake her hand warmly in both of his. "Annaya, I presume. Thank you so much for coming. I'm sorry for all the formality. It must seem strange. Please, come with me. A cup of tea will help you relax after that long flight."

"Oh... thank you," Annaya replied bewilderedly.

She'd been expecting him to fly into her with a long rant about her promiscuous behavior or to be called a gold-digger, but the man before her seemed nothing like Jack had described. He was calm and hospitable and quick to offer her a cup of tea when they came to rest in a beautiful and ornate tea room towards the back of the mansion.

Annaya sat down nervously on the edge of a golden

chintz sofa with elaborately carved legs and anxiously took a sip from her cup. She wondered where Jack was and felt very uneasy to be left alone with his father, although Brandon was smiling at her reassuringly.

"No need to look so afraid, my dear."

"Jack had asked me to keep the whole thing quiet," Annaya confessed. "I thought you'd be unhappy to see me here."

"Jack has never been the best at confronting his errors. I'm just sorry it took this long for the matter to reach a resolution. I'm grateful, in fact, that you were discreet about the whole matter and that you came so promptly."

"Of course. I'm sorry that this happened in the first

place. I know how important your reputation is. I promise you, I had no idea who Jack was when I met him. This was never my intention."

"I believe that. If you were after his money, I'm sure we'd have known about it by now."

"I don't want his money."

"What *do* you want from my son?"

Annaya was taken aback and looked at Brandon with round, surprised eyes. "Nothing."

"Nothing?"

"Nothing. It's more about what Jack wants. This is his child, too."

"Jack thought I'd be angry to hear about what had happened, but I'll confess, that I actually think the situation could end up working out for all of us. Jack has a reputation as a 'playboy'." The billionaire's expression of disapproval returned to his face at the word and Annaya could tell that he was not a fan of that description. He sighed heavily before continuing his explanation. "I believe that in the past he has enjoyed that reputation and done his best to live up to it.

I want nothing more than for him to settle down and step up to his responsibilities. This pregnancy could be a blessing in disguise. Jack tells me that nobody knows about how you met and I can soon arrange for casino footage of that night to be destroyed so that it stays that way. Jack has a real chance here to reinvent himself as a family man."

"A family man?"

"Yes. A child could be just what is needed to pull him away from all that nonsense and help him focus on what matters. Still, I'm confusing you. I think it's perhaps best that you see Jack now. He'll make it all clear."

Brandon was right. Annaya was confused. The billionaire was speaking so cryptically, as though he had some trick up his sleeve that he was about to reveal to her. Annaya wondered what it was. What role was the billionaire expecting her to play? What lies were they planning to spin? How were they going to avert this PR disaster?

The billionaire gestured for her to follow him and he led her out of the tea room to another room on the other side of the mansion. They came to a stop at a grand oak door and Brandon stepped back with a smile on his face. "Jack's waiting for you. Go ahead."

Uncertainly, Annaya stepped forward and pushed open the door. She gasped at what she saw inside and let the heavy door slam shut behind her, closing off her and Jack in a room that was filled with roses and lit by candles. The scent of so many flowers made Annaya's head spin, as did the sight of Jack in a suit, down on one knee and holding up a little black velvet box which contained the biggest diamond engagement ring that she had ever seen. He was smiling, but looked as nervous and uncertain as she did.

"Annaya," he began, clearing his throat slightly, "I know this isn't the conventional way to do things and that we don't know each other all that well. I know that you've got a life in California and I've no right to expect you to drop everything for a man who's hardly more than a stranger. I know that all of this is crazy, but I promised I'd support you and I meant it, so that is why, Annie, I want to ask you if you'll do me the honor of being my wife. Will you marry me?"

Chapter 7

At first, Annaya stared at Jack in complete shock and then a laugh rose up in her throat and she shook her head in disbelief. "Stand up, Jack. Don't be ridiculous."

Jack frowned and slowly picked himself up from the ground. "I'm trying to do the right thing."

"The right thing? You're being insane. We hardly know each other. What was this – your father's idea?"

"He's right, Annaya. I need to start stepping up and settling down. We've got a baby on the way. A marriage makes sense. Why not?"

"'Why not'? Because I'm not going to marry someone

for appearances, that's why not. Jesus, Jack, are you mad?"

"I'm sorry. I thought a commitment was what you were looking for."

"A commitment as a father. That doesn't mean I expect you to drop everything and be my husband. What kind of marriage would that be? Just on paper? This is the craziest thing I've ever heard of. I can't believe you just did that."

Jack's face reddened slightly at her reaction and he placed the engagement ring back in his pocket and gave a nonchalant shrug. "I thought all women were after marriage."

"You were wrong."

Annaya was in complete shock and her head was

spinning. She couldn't believe Jack had proposed to her. She knew that he had undoubtedly done it to please his father and ensure he wasn't disowned for stepping out of line for the last time, but all the same, she found the situation absurd and gave him another stern frown and shook her head.

Did she want to get married? Of course, someday. Did she want to marry Jack? She wanted to marry someone like Jack, certainly. She wanted someone handsome, smart and wealthy, but there was no matter how handsome, smart or wealthy, Annaya had been waiting for love and she wasn't about to settle now for convenience. She had more dignity than that.

"So, what now?" she asked him, stepping over to one of those beautiful bouquets and taking a deep breath of its sweet scent. "We're not getting married, so does that mean I'm going home? Will I see you again?"

"Of course you'll see me again. As for the fine print, I just don't know. Perhaps you could stay a while and we'll figure it all out."

"Stay a while?"

Annaya raised her eyebrows and looked up at the high ceilings and around at the beautiful decor and she could imagine enjoying being surrounded by this kind of luxury, but she knew that time with Jack here would be no holiday. His proposal had been rejected and now his father was involved and the whole situation was just a bit strange.

Still, Annaya had just travelled all this way and she didn't want to turn on her heel and leave again so soon. Plus, she wanted to know what happened next.

She had so many unanswered questions. Ever since this whole thing had begun, she and Jack had been skipping around the details of their situation, but the time was drawing closer where he and Annaya had to start making plans.

What would they do in terms of custody? Where would the child go to school? How would they arrange the child support? Annaya didn't want to leave those details to chance or think of them as distant, irrelevant things to worry about when the time came. She was worrying about them *now* and wanted to know that Jack would be there.

"Fine," she said at last with a heavy sigh, "but only because we have things to discuss."

"I'll take you to my place across town. You don't want to stay here with my father."

"No. He seems to have his own ideas for how this whole thing should go."

"That's my father."

"I'll grab my bags."

*****

Jack knew he'd made a huge mistake in proposing to Annaya and now things would probably be incredibly awkward for them both, but the surprising woman had seemed to have taken his moment of insanity in stride and quickly brushed it aside. But now it was back to the real matters at hand.

Why had he done it? His father's influence, certainly, but also because when he was around Annaya, the thought of settling down didn't seem nearly so oppressive. Annaya surprised him constantly. She was beautiful, strong, and level-headed. Perhaps the love of a good woman was exactly what he needed in his life.

The billionaire shook his head at his own foolishness and sighed. If he'd ever had a chance with her he was sure he'd blown it now. He'd thrown her life off course by getting her pregnant in the first place and had then tried to solve the problem by throwing more insanity his way. He was sure there was no way she'd be able to think of him now as anything other than an impulsive and reckless playboy who'd do anything to stay in his father's good books.

There were a hundred things he wished he'd done differently at this point and he was starting to realize Annaya meant more to him that just a one-night stand. She was the only woman who'd ever held his attention and now she was to be the mother of his child. And already he'd screwed it all up. There was nothing left to do than to step up to the mark in whatever way Annaya needed and hope that she'd forgive him for panicking.

*****

Jack's own property was huge, although not quite as large as where his father lived. It was slightly on the outskirts of the city in grounds of its own and was only one-story high, although that one story covered a huge expanse of space. Unlike his father's mansion, which was manor-like and old-fashioned, Jack's home was filled with modern technology, and black, white and chrome decor.

He lead her into his living room, which had a pristine white carpet, black leather sofas and a huge ornamental electric fireplace and he told her to put her bags down wherever she wanted.

"Your place is beautiful."

"Thanks."

There was a moment of silence. Since they'd met, there'd been surprisingly few awkward silences, considering the circumstances, but since Jack's proposal that morning, they'd had almost nothing to say to one another, despite Annaya's attempts to pretend it had never happened.

After a short while of uncomfortable lingering, Jack sighed deeply and stepped across the room to stand in front of Annaya. Even though he'd done something mad that morning and Annaya had no idea what to expect of him next, she still couldn't stop herself feeling the way she did around him -- weak-kneed and breathless.

She'd seen him look embarrassed for the first time today and it had been like seeing Caesar fall, but it humanized him also, and let Annaya know that she wasn't the only one who had no idea what she was doing. Jack took hold of her hands and looked in her eyes with a mixture of regret and apology in his own.

"I'm sorry for what I did this morning, Annaya," he said sincerely. "It was a moment of panic. I was trying to step up and thought it was the right thing to do. I realize now that a woman like you doesn't want a quick fix. A woman like you would rather do it right, in her own time. You're incredibly strong, Annaya, and I should have known better than to think you needed a man to propose to you for you to be alright. I know you're plenty strong enough on your own."

Annaya's smiled softened and she gave his hands a grateful little squeeze. "Thank you for saying that, Jack. Let's just forget about the whole thing, shall we? I can't blame you for having a moment of madness. God knows I've had no idea what I've been doing since this whole thing began. Your heart was in the right place... I think."

"It was. I know you imagine that I was simply steam-rolled by my father, but I promise you, Annaya, he's tried to get me to settle down many times before and I've only ever laughed at the idea. I've always considered myself something of a lone wolf, a free spirit – I don't know – but when I'm with you, I could imagine being the kind of family man my father wants me to be. Perhaps one day."

"Perhaps."

The way he spoke made Annaya's heart start fluttering again and he was looking at her with such tenderness in his eyes, as though there were feelings beneath the words, although Annaya refused to believe that he could feel anything for her under the circumstances. But, then again, didn't she feel weak at the knees every time she saw him and didn't she long for her Thursday nights when they could speak and she felt like everything would be alright?

It wasn't love – not yet – but something was growing between them, something building from that spark that had ignited the moment they'd met. Annaya prayed that it would be smooth sailing from here on out and that they'd find their way somehow. She wanted Jack to stick around, whatever happened, but she hoped that his proposal would be his last moment of madness and that now they could move forward in their own way and in good time.

*****

Jack held Annaya's hand as they walked through the mall. It wasn't as glamorous as that glitzy night they'd first met, but Annaya still felt that same feeling of privilege and excitement to be holding his hand in public, knowing that every woman must be looking at him with hungry eyes, wishing they were in her place.

It made her feel like she was still wearing that clingy dress with her perfect figure in a luxurious place. Jack had suggested getting out for a while and they'd ended up agreeing to go to the mall to look at some baby items together for the first time.

"I've got no idea what the baby will need," Jack confessed, "so you'll have to make a list."

"The basics will do."

"No. I want my child to have the best."

"He or she won't know any different. They'll be a baby."

"That's not the point."

"I didn't grow up with a silver spoon in my mouth and I survived."

Jack threw her a smile and Annaya smiled back. Every now and then, their difference in status would come up in one way or another and Annaya would always try and make a point of her independence and non-reliance on the material things. She was proud of the fact that she'd done so much on her own, and she wanted her child to have the same grit and determination.

"There's nothing wrong with an upper-class upbringing," Jack chastised gently. "I went to private school and had holidays in Europe and it did me no harm, either."

"Really? Because you weren't behaving the night that we met."

"Neither of us were."

They grinned at each other. That one night kept coming up again and again; the night where it all began, and despite all the chaos that had come from it, they both remembered it with fondness as the night that they both realized for the first time that this mysterious thing that other people called a "spark" or "chemistry" really did exist and really was powerful.

Annaya threaded her arm through Jack's so that she was walking closer to him. It felt so natural to walk with him that way and occasionally, it crossed her mind that perhaps she should avoid acting so much like a couple with him when they still hadn't established what they really were at all. But she just couldn't help herself when he was so close to her that all she had to do was reach out and thread her arm through his.

"Do you want a boy or a girl?" she asked him absently.

Jack smiled at her question. "Have you been thinking about it?"

"Haven't you?"

"It still doesn't feel real, even after all this time. I've not let myself think about all the details too much."

"Our baby will be here before you know it, Jack. It's time to start thinking about these things."

"Well, if we're thinking about these things, then I suppose I like the idea of a boy. You know, a little Jack to throw a ball around with or to teach all I know."

Annaya laughed lightly. "Throw a ball around with? Jack, I can't believe that you've ever played sports in your life."

"That's not true!" Jack exclaimed, in mock-offence. "I was a brilliant lacrosse player." His tone was half-serious, but his eyes were completely playful when he shot her a sideways glance and a teasing smile. "No, you're right, I wasn't the most boisterous child, but I wasn't allowed to be. I'd love to do all those things with a son that I wish my father had done with me."

"You're not close to your father, are you?"

"The problem is, I aspire too much to be like my father and he equally aspires too much that I should follow in his footsteps, when the fact is, we are entirely different people and I am never going to do all that he has done."

"Do you have to?"

"There's a certain expectation that comes with a prestigious family name. I have big shoes to fill."

"And if you have a son, will you expect him to follow in your footsteps?"

"If I have a son, he can be whatever he wants to be."

"And if you have a daughter?"

"A daughter?" Jack chuckled at the thought. "Well, I can't really imagine me finding it coming all too natural to take care of a little girl, but, if I had a daughter, and she was anything like her mother, I know I'd adore her."

Annaya both loved and hated those thinly-veiled compliments that Jack threw into their conversations, because they both delighted and confused her. It sent little shivers of joy down her spine whenever Jack said she was beautiful or whenever he admired her in any other way, because Jack's compliments made her feel incredible, but at the same time, they left her wondering what it all meant. Was a compliment just a compliment, or was it a hint at something more?

"Well, I'd like a daughter," she told him firmly. "I want a little girl to do all those mother-daughter things that I did with my mother and sister. There's no bond like the bond between a mother and her little girl."

"Ah yes, your mother. I've yet to meet them. My offer still stands."

"I know," Annaya said gratefully. "I'm building up to it."

"You're scared they won't like me?"

"I don't know what I'm scared of, Jack. I suppose that once they're involved, there's no hiding from it anymore."

"You don't need to hide. We're going to be OK."

Jack made a sudden beeline for a baby shop and began to stroll around the aisles in a slightly bewildered daze, while Annaya felt herself grow broody and excited. She picked up a little tiny pair of knitted pink booties and felt herself turn to mush.

"Look at these, Jack!" she exclaimed. "Aren't they *adorable*?"

"Very cute."

"And this little babygro! Oh my God! *Look at those tiny little feet*!"

Jack laughed. He'd never seen Annaya act like a girly-girl before, turning to coo over puppies or babies, but it made him smile to know that she had a softer side too. She was always so strong and independent that from time to time he found it easy to forget that there was vulnerability and a softness beneath the confident sexuality and strong mind.

They spent the next few hours strolling from one store to the other, letting their collection of baby goods grow, until at last they arrived back at Jack's apartment with dozens of bags and tired feet.

Annaya looked around at everything they'd bought and laughed. "I didn't expect to go so mad with it," she confessed.

"It makes me feel better to know that you have the things you need."

"Thank you for today, Jack. It's just what I needed. A day to look forward to the baby and not worry about it for a change."

"Are you worried?"

"Aren't you?"

Jack came to sit beside her on the sofa and let one arm rest on the back of the sofa behind Annaya's head. He smiled at her and shook his head, "No."

"You're not worried at all?"

"Should I be?"

"You're going to be a father."

"I've got a great mother at my side to help me get through."

There he went again with those compliments that drove Annaya mad. What was he trying to say? She tried to divert the conversation.

"Is it alright if I take a bath? All that walking did me in."

"Sure. Go ahead."

Annaya smiled at him and headed into his enormous bathroom with its marble floors and polished granite tub. The whole bath was lined with bulbs that glowed blue under the water and there were candles on the windowsill. Annaya lighted one and smiled at the floral scent it released. She was surprised to find these feminine touches at Jack's place and wondered if it was for his benefit or the benefit of the women he brought home.

She didn't like to think about the other women in Jack's life. She was sure there had been many. She knew she couldn't be jealous or complain, because, after all, if she hadn't gotten pregnant, she would have been just another notch on his bedpost, and he would have been just another notch on hers.

It was funny how life worked sometimes. It was supposed to have been a one-night stand to lead her thoughts away from how everyone around her had their lives in order, but all it had done was send her own life even further out of control. Although chaos didn't feel so bad in a billionaire's bathroom, soaking in lavender-scented water by the flickering light of pillar candles.

She wished that every day felt as carefree as this one, but she only ever felt relaxed around Jack. He simply had a calming effect on her, perhaps because he was always so calm himself and because he had so much faith in her.

Annaya sank down in the bath and felt her sore and aching muscles unwind. She leaned her head back against the marble and relished the feeling of the water lapping against her bare skin. She didn't even hear Jack come in, but she sensed him standing there and her eyes flew open. She gasped when she spotted him and went to sit up to cover herself, but Jack turned his eyes away with a little laugh.

"Sorry, Annie. You forgot your towel. I did knock."

The startled woman noticed the towel in his hand and she smiled. "Thanks."

"I'll just put it down here."

*****

Jack kept his eyes averted as he put the towel down and made it almost entirely out of the room before he made the fatal mistake of looking back. God, she was beautiful. A brief glance was all it took to make all his logic vanish and his urges rise up. Everything about her was perfection, from her smooth, dark skin, to her wild hair which was now wet and dripping around her sweet face, to her pert, round breasts with dark nipples. Once he had glanced, he couldn't help but stare, and once he started staring, he couldn't help but get caught.

Annaya blushed when she saw him staring and for a moment Jack thought that she would tell him to leave, but when she didn't, he took it as an invitation to draw closer and sit on the edge of the tub. The woman who drove him mad drove him even more crazy when she looked up at him from the tub with round, alluring eyes, widened slightly from surprise and anticipation with one hand half-covering one breast in the barest attempt at concealing herself.

The billionaire sat on the edge of the tub and began to

run his hand through the warm water, sending waves lapping against Annaya's thighs. His eyes followed their current, watching how the water brushed against her clear, soft skin, covering between her legs, but only enveloping half of her breasts, which rose out of the water like eager mountains awaiting him. He felt himself growing hard at the sight of her and his hand wandered down between her legs.

Annaya watched him breathlessly as he began to rub his palm against her and then slip a finger inside. The feeling of him teasing her and the warm water swirling made her bite down on her lip and that drove Jack over the edge. Not caring that he'd get wet, he submerged both arms into the water to scoop her up and carry her into the bedroom. He threw her down on the bed and lapped up lavender droplets from her breasts.

She was so beautiful naked, especially when Jack could see how much she wanted him. At first she'd seemed surprised that he'd touched her, but now she seemed to have given into her own desires and let go of her own inhibitions; swept up in that same wave of attraction that made Jack throw all his own logic out the window.

He tore off his now-dripping shirt, his pants and underpants and moved on top of her. Her body was still warm and damp from the bath water and his body slid effortlessly against hers as he entered her and began to thrust. They began to make love wildly, passionately and without hesitation, saving all their doubts for later, when the cry of each other's bodies wasn't demanding that they give in once again.

*****

"What do you mean 'nothing happened'? You've been gone for two weeks!"

Annaya laughed at Natalie's wide-eyed exclamation and took a sip from her tea. It was true. What was meant to have been a couple of days of talking through the fine-print with Jack had turned into a couple of weeks of talking things through and getting to know each other better. The awkwardness between them had faded after Jack's apology and then, just like things seemed to always happen between them, the intensity had built and built until it was time to say goodbye and they were back at square one.

"We talked. We made some decisions. He showed me some more of Vegas – the parts that aren't in casinos."

"And?"

"And what?"

"You know what I mean. How were things between you two? Are you friends now, or something more?"

Annaya sighed deeply and gave a morose shrug. "I honestly don't know, Nat. There are times when I think there's something between us. Jack says things sometimes that make me wonder if he's got feelings for me, but then we end up taking a step back. I think that with the baby on the way, we're both just afraid of ending up together for the wrong reasons. It's hard to tell if we have feelings for each other, or are just excited about the pregnancy and are letting that take over."

"Are you serious?" Natalie said irritably. "Annaya, you've got a reputation for never letting a man get close to you. You're the pickiest person I know, but

234

whenever you talk about that man, you practically swoon. Pregnancy or not, you've got feelings for that man."

"And even if I do, what am I supposed to do with them?" Annaya sighed. She lifted her head and looked out of the coffee shop window longingly at the little family outside: mother, father and baby in its pram. She dreamed of having a scene like that in her own life one day, but she had no idea how things would go with her and Jack and whether they'd ever act like a family. Annaya paused for a moment and then looked back at Natalie with a serious expression. "He proposed to me."

"*What*?" Natalie exclaimed, splashing coffee over the counter as she jolted at the news. She looked around at all the people who'd looked up at the sound of her crying out and then she lowered her voice and leaned in closer to Annaya to continue their conversation.

"'Nothing happened'! He proposed to you. That's a pretty big something, in my books. What did you say?"

"What do you mean, what did I say? I said no, of course. I hardly know the man."

"Do you think that's for the best?"

"What are you saying, Natalie? You think I should have married the man?"

"You could do worse."

"Are you serious? Sure, Jack's a catch in a lot of ways, but just because he ticks some boxes on paper, doesn't mean that he'd make a good husband. Anything you do in a panic, will only end in tears. If I ever married Jack, it would be because I loved him and he loved me, and not just because we're both trying to do the right thing."

"I admire you, Annaya, but I think you're mad," Natalie confessed. "You've been going on a lot lately about how you're getting older and last chances and all that, and a gorgeous man who wants to take care of you offers to marry you and you turn him down? I know it didn't start in the most sensible of ways, but crazier things have happened than a one-night stand turning out to be something really good."

"I'm trying to keep my head here, Nat. Look at him. Jack has everything. He's handsome, rich, intelligent and has women all over him. He's practically a celebrity. Why would a big shot like him settle down with a nobody? I won't marry him just to spin some good PR."

Natalie sighed, looked over at her friend with tender admiration and gave a reassuring smile. "I'm sorry. You're right. Do what you feel is right."

That was easier said than done. What felt right was becoming Mrs. Annaya Casali, but every logical part of her being told her that that was insane. Ever since leaving Vegas this time Annaya had been kept awake at night with ceaseless thoughts of 'what if?'. What if she'd said yes? Would she be planning her own wedding now? Would she be buying her gown? Would she bowled over by her mother's hugs when she informed her she'd bagged a billionaire?

It was all well and good fantasizing about what could have been if Annaya had said yes instead of no, but she'd made up her mind. There were too many unknowns for her to rush into something like that with a man she barely knew. She wouldn't marry Jack unless everything was right.

Chapter8

Annaya was a mess of nerves as Jack pulled up outside her parent's house that Wednesday afternoon. Jack saw how flustered she was growing, tugging at the seatbelt that was digging into her now swollen belly and shooting nervous glances up the driveway and he smiled and calmly lay his hand on her knee.

"What are you so nervous about, Annie? I thought you wanted me to meet them."

"I do," Annaya said uncertainly. "It's just that it's such a weird situation already and I don't want it to get any worse..."

"Get any worse?" Jack repeated with a little chuckle. He raised his eyebrows at her. "Am I that bad?"

"Hmm, let's see," Annaya began sarcastically, listing their antics on her fingers with a little frown. "We had a shotgun drunken wedding in Vegas, followed by an equally quick annulment, only to find out I was pregnant, which led to you proposing again, despite how great the first wedding turned out to be..."

"You said you wouldn't mention the proposal again," Jack scolded with a little half-laugh. He gave her another patient and reassuring smile. "It's all going to be fine. Besides, I should be the nervous one."

"You're right. You should be."

Despite Jack's offer to meet her parents months before, it took until Annaya's seventh month of pregnancy before she felt brave enough to introduce him to them. She wanted to avoid their judgment for as long as possible and to keep Jack out of the firing line. Just like Brandon Casali, her parents had their own views of the right way to proceed, and she didn't want Jack to be scolded by them.

Her parents were conservative, upstanding members of the community who had expected Annaya to get married to a nice man, settle down in a family home and have children in that order, and instead she'd found herself getting everything quite muddled up and she worried about what they'd think of the man who was to blame.

Not that Annaya blamed him, of course. From the start she'd known that it had taken both of them to make a baby and she couldn't fault Jack in all the ways he'd stepped up to the mark when she'd told him she was pregnant. He'd been there with her at Natalie's wedding and then on the phone with her once a week ever since and supported her financially and emotionally all the way up to that awful moment in Vegas where he'd proposed out-of-the-blue.

They'd both decided to put that day behind them and they hadn't spoken about it again, although every now and then Annaya would find herself wondering again about whether she'd made the wrong choice in turning him down. Every time she saw Jack, it seemed, she wanted to be closer to him, and be with him longer and just generally have him near her for as long and as close as possible. Instead, she had brief visits with him here and there are long conversations on the phone, but it just wasn't enough to make her feel satisfied.

She wanted desperately to be with him all the time, but she just didn't know how to make that happen without drawing him into a trap. After all, how many conversations had Annaya heard from men talking about the dangers of a woman entrapping a man with a child? She didn't want to be counted among them, especially as Jack was a rich man and it was just another reason for people to point a finger at her and label her as a man eater and a gold-digger.

No, as much as she wanted to be with him, she felt that there was no way to do it that would seem right. Even though they were seven months into this now, they still didn't know each other as well as they should, and she didn't know how she could confess that she had feelings for him and make it sound true – even though it was.

She looked him over now as they sat in the car. He was wearing an expensive pair of denim blue jeans and a pristine off-white shirt with very faint

pinstripes. The top button of his collar was open,

exposing the bottom of his throat and just a glimpse

of his strong, firm chest. His hair was slightly

windswept from having the car window just slightly

open on the way here from her apartment, where he'd

picked her up, and he was clean-shaven for the

occasion. He looked as lean and handsome and

immaculate as ever and Annaya felt stupid knowing

that she was harboring feelings for him now, because

how could he have any feelings for her?

Annaya wasn't attractive any more. At least, she

wasn't sexy. Her stomach had swollen far more than

she'd expected it to, so that when she was standing up

straight she couldn't even see her toes and she had to

stand leaning backward with her hands pressing into

her spine to help support her own weight. She

waddled now, rather than glided and no matter how much make-up she put on, she couldn't stop her cheeks from shining pink.

She was far removed from the vision that had attracted him in the club, all fluttering eyelashes and sex appeal. Now she was a waddling frump and she wondered if Jack resented her being around. But if he did resent her, or blame her, or hate the situation, he did a good job of hiding it. He always had a smile ready for her, even after a flight from Vegas or on the way to meet her parents.

Today they'd gone for another scan and had finally decided that they wanted to know the gender of the baby. They were having a little girl. Annaya didn't know what she'd expected to see in Jack when he'd heard the news, but she was surprised to see a big smile spread across his face when the midwife announced it. Jack was rather good at keeping his emotions in check and living under that playboy persona, so it was always a surprise to see the facade break and the man beneath showing his feelings. Jack had told her that he was thrilled they were having a daughter and, the way he'd smiled when he'd said it and gripped onto her hand with bright eyes, Annaya had believed him.

*****

Every time Jack had to leave Bakersfield, it was harder and harder to do. He'd grown up in the largest and most luxurious of houses, being given everything he could have ever wanted, but he never felt torn when stepping out of his mansion or away from the bright lights of Vegas.

No, he felt most like he was leaving home when he stepped away from Annaya, with her dazzling smile and chipped coffee mugs, in her cozy little apartment. He felt at ease with her in a way he didn't with anyone else in the world and every time he left her, he missed her.

She was beautiful to him, even now. He'd first been attracted to a woman with big, mysterious eyes and a body to die for, but now there were different things about her that attracted him even more; like the sound of her laugh and that pregnant glow on her cheeks. He found the little whistling sound she made when she finally sat down in a chair after waddling a short way to be adorable and of course, her dazzling smile was just as it had always been.

His feelings for the woman were growing. He

admired Annaya more than he could say. She was strong, capable and unwilling to back down for anybody, which was impressive. When she'd turned down his proposal at his father's mansion, he'd been shocked initially.

Ever since he'd hit puberty, the press had advertised him as the most eligible bachelor around and he'd had women throwing themselves at him when he was in his teens and so he'd felt a moment of shock when Annie had laughed and told him to get off his knees.

Looking back, it had been a terrible idea. Jack thought it through before the proposal and had imagined that a marriage would help give a good impression in the short-term and if it didn't work out long-term... well, that's what divorce was for. His mistake had been forgetting that Annaya wasn't the cynic that he was.

She believed in love and craved it. She wasn't after his money and she was a frail, fragile thing that needed the protection of a man through the ties of marriage. Annaya couldn't be bought and that's why Jack was mad about her. She'd turned down his proposal, and yet returned every one of his longing glances. She felt something for him, he knew, but the question was how to turn it into something more.

Meeting her parents may very well be a good start, he thought – or a disaster. He wasn't in the habit of being brought home to meet a girl's folks, but back in Vegas, he supposed it wasn't necessary. Parents would have killed for their daughters to be chosen by such a wealthy and influential man. Annaya, however, had parents who had raised a defiant and

independent young woman, and he was sure that if
Annaya was anything to go by, then her parents
would be hard to impress.

*****

Annaya saw Jack looking around at the small
property with its slightly overgrown garden and that
one wonky shutter and wondered what he really
thought of them. There were no chandeliers here, no
crystals or champagne. Annaya and her parents were
just ordinary people from an ordinary background
and, for some reason, Annaya felt much more nervous
to have Jack step into her world, than she'd ever felt
stepping into his. She felt exposed here, like he could
see all her secrets. She looked up at his gorgeous face
and her doubts melted away. He stepped closer to her
and casually laid a hand to rest on the small of her

back. Annaya took a deep breath and rang the doorbell.

Her mother was the one to open the door. She was a stout, matronly Nigerian woman with lips that could produce either a dazzling smile like Annaya's own, or the most lethal scowl. Right now, her expression couldn't make up its mind which to produce and instead she fixed Jack with a stern, judgmental stare, slowly running her gaze up and down the body of the billionaire.

"This is the one, hmm?" she announced at last. She pointed a wagging finger at Jack disapprovingly. "You have left my daughter in a difficult position. I was not pleased to hear it. Did you not think what your little night of fun might do?"

"Mrs. Towler, I am incredibly sorry for everything,"

Jack said with a sincere expression on his face. "It was never my intention to leave your daughter in this position and I assure you that she will have everything she needs from this point forwards. Everything."

Annaya's mother, Shona, gave a reluctant nod and, even though her lips were still pursed, she stepped back to let the pair in, pausing only briefly to plant a kiss on Annaya's cheek.

"Seven months!" Shona declared as she led them into the lounge. "It took seven months to meet the man. Where were you, boy, hiding?"

Annie wished that the ground would swallow her up when her mother called Jack 'boy', but the billionaire seemed to appreciate Shona's motherly protectiveness and he just smiled a small smile of amusement before remembering he was supposed to look repentant and plastered a more serious expression on his face.

"I'm very sorry again, Mrs. Towler. There's a flight between us and I work very long hours."

"What are you? Some businessman?"

They were in the lounge now, where Annaya's father was reclining in his sagging old armchair, half-asleep. He was growing frail in his older years and his once-black curly hair was now a shocking white, but his wrinkles had given him a much kindlier expression than the stern one that Annaya remembered from her youth. Drake Towler had mellowed a lot in his old age and rather than attacking Jack, as Shona had done, he simply stood and extended a hand to him.

"It is good to meet you at last. Jack, is it?"

"Yes, sir."

"Drake. And I see you've met my wife, Shona."

"This businessman reckons he is too busy to be flying over to take care of our daughter."

"A man's got to put food on the table, Shona. Come in Jack, sit."

Drake beckoned for Jack to enter the room and gestured for him to take a seat. Jack thanked him and sat down on the mint-green and pink striped sofa that the couple had in their lounge since the seventies and he accepted a cup of tea from Shona, who was still muttering to herself about this Vegas businessman who wasn't taking proper care of her daughter.

At last, all four were sitting in the lounge, drinking tea and looking around at one another, until Jack

255

broke the silence.

"You have quite an incredible daughter," he said. Annaya didn't know if he was still buttering her parents up, but he sounded sincere and she dipped her head to hide a smile. "I've been amazed with how she'd reacted to this whole thing. She's a very strong woman."

"Of course she is!" Shona declared proudly. "She takes after her mother."

"Annaya has always had her head screwed on right," Drake added. "A straight-A student at school. A hard-worker now. Always very independent. When her friends were out chasing boys, she was out causing trouble. A tomboy, when she was young, she was. You wouldn't know it to look at her now, of course."

"No," Jack agreed. "She's stunning."

The billionaire shot her a sideways glance that made Annaya blush again. Every time he spoke fondly of her with a compliment or comment about her strength or how he admired her, she couldn't help but believe him. She wanted to reach out and hold onto his hand, but it felt wrong with her parents watching and judging them.

After an awkward beginning, and a lot of questioning from Shona, it seemed that Jack eventually won the pair over with his smooth talking and sincere promises to do right by Annaya and when at last they left, Annaya felt like a huge weight had been lifted from her shoulders.

"Thank you, Jack," she said. "It means a lot to me that you met them."

"How'd I do?"

"I think they like you."

"Well, I guess now we've both met each other's parents and they both kind-of approve. That's something, I suppose."

"I don't think any of them approve," Annaya laughed lightly, "but there's no secrets anymore, and that's a start. We'll win them over in time."

"You're right," Jack agreed. "And for now, we have something much more important to worry about."

"What's that?"

"We have to think of a name for our little girl."

That was perhaps the very moment that Annaya realized she was truly in love with Jack Casali. With everything around them so stressful and demanding and nothing going right, Jack was able to bring everything back to a reason to be joyful. He was a man who didn't shirk his responsibilities and who didn't expect her to change to fit into his world.

She felt like they were made for each other, but there was no way to say that without it sounding incredible corny, or like a woman who regretted not saying yes to a tempting proposal simply changing her mind.

Jack came back to her apartment after their afternoon with her parents to wait for his evening flight. She made them both some tea and they sat down on her sofa side by side, beginning to go over some logistics for the birth and for afterwards.

"I'm due July 21st," Annaya told him. "Will you be here?"

"I'll be wherever you need me to be. You have my number."

"The baby could come early, or late, or just on time. I want you to be there, Jack."

Jack reached over and squeezed her hand. "I will be."

"I hate that you're in Vegas."

There, she said it. It had been on the tip of her tongue for months and finally she'd come out and said it. How much easier it would be if Jack was there with her all the time! How much calmer she'd feel knowing he was a drive away, rather than a flight.

How much more willing she'd be to give into her feelings if she had even half a chance of it going somewhere. She didn't want the father of her child to be so far away. She wanted him to be here, a part of their lives.

Jack smiled understandingly and held her hand. "I hate it too, actually. I don't want to miss out on anything."

"You should stay here around the time the baby's due," Annaya said. "Then you'd be here, no matter what."

"You said yourself, Annie, the baby could come at any time. I can't be away from the business for that long. Besides, I don't think you should have the baby here."

"What do you mean?"

"I want you to have the best. I could arrange for you to stay in Vegas and have staff on call for when you went into labor. I could get you in with the best doctors in a private hospital. You would have much better care."

Annaya let out a hollow laugh. "I don't want to have my baby in Vegas, Jack. I want my family around me. How would my mother feel if she couldn't see her grandchild after I'd given birth? I'll be having the baby here, Jack."

Jack sighed heavily. "Fine, but I'm pulling some strings to make sure you get the best here."

"I don't care about any of that," Annaya insisted. "I just want you to promise you'll be there when she's born."

"I'll drop everything the moment you call," Jack replied. "I promise."

It wasn't really good enough, but Annaya felt like she

was better taking what she could get than starting a row when she wouldn't change Jack's mind. This is what it always came down to with the two of them: logistics. He'd want to be in Vegas, she'd want to be here, and they'd both worry so much about what the whole thing would look like to everyone else that they never made any decisions at all.

She laid her head against his shoulder, weary suddenly from the stress of having so much to think about. Jack laid his cheek against the top of her head and they leaned against each other a while for strength and then, suddenly, Jack raised his head and turned Annaya's face towards him. He looked deeply into her eyes and shook his head slowly as if he was amazed by the sight.

"You're so beautiful, Annie." He leaned forward to

kiss her and for the briefest moment, his rough lips brushed against her soft ones, before Annaya pressed her hands against his chest and pushed him away.

"Don't, Jack."

"Why not, Annie? You look so beautiful right now."

"Because we'll do what we've done before. We'll get caught up in the moment, have sex and then go our separate ways until next time. All the while, I'll be wondering if there's really anything between us, only to know that it doesn't really matter anyway, because everything else is getting in the way."

"What are you trying to say?"

"I'm saying that it's got to be all or nothing, Jack," Annaya said firmly. "Think about it. We've got our whole lives ahead of us. How would you feel if I met a man, but was sleeping with you every time you flew

over? Or worse still, what if I never met anyone

because I was sleeping with you, but you and me

never really got anywhere? I don't want to be on my

own, Jack, but unless we sort ourselves out and

whatever *this* is, that's what's going to happen. I need

some clarity so that I can plan my life. I don't want to

just be someone you screw when you're in town."

Jack let out an offended breath and sat back from her.

"Is that what you think of me, Annie? That I'm just

hanging about for the chance to get laid? I haven't got

any trouble filling my bed."

Annaya rolled her eyes at the way he said it, as if she

should be impressed. "Maybe that's the point. You

take it all for granted. Me, some other woman – what

does it matter to you? The great Jack Casali can have

anyone he wants."

"That's not fair. I've been there for you ever since this all started."

"But what do you *want*, Jack?" Annaya asked exasperatedly. "I'm waiting for you to tell me that I mean something to you and that you want more, but we just let it build up and build up and then you fly away and it fizzles out until next time. That's not how I want to live my life."

"I offered you a commitment, Annie, and you turned me down. How dare you act like I've not done all I can!"

"You only proposed to me because your Daddy told you to."

Jack's face flushed red and he stood up with a

scowl, picking up his jacket and his bag from her sitting room and heading towards the door. He turned back on his heel at the last minute as though he were going to say something to her, but then just shook his head in a mute fury and walked away. After he'd left, Annaya buried her head in her hands and burst into tears. He was gone again.

Chapter 9

The first labor pains came as Annaya was attempting to walk to the corner store to buy some chocolate for her cravings. At first, she assumed that the shooting pains through her abdomen were just signs of exertion. After all, over the last couple of months she'd grown bigger and bigger and had consequently moved around less and less and so a journey to the local shops was almost a marathon to her.

She ignored the first few pains and told herself it was just due to the exercise, but she couldn't explain it away when two hours later her waters broke in the middle of the main street to the horror of shocked people who passed by.

For the first time since this all began, Annaya felt real fear. Up until this point, she'd felt unprepared and a little in shock and certainly anxious, but it was as the cramps began to tighten around her middle and she knew that the baby was well and truly on its way that she began to really grow frightened of what would come next.

She was about to become a single mother – or as good as – and the baby's father was all the way in Vegas probably playing at some roulette wheel or another, and they'd hardly spoken in weeks, apart from short, angry sentences on the phone.

Jack was mad at her for the way she'd spoken to him and she was angry with him because he hadn't fought harder to keep her. Annaya was so messed up from the pregnancy hormones and the confusion of it all, that she had no idea who was in the wrong anymore.

Perhaps she shouldn't have pushed his buttons the way she had done that night. All she'd wanted was for him to tell her that he felt the same and to convince him to stay, but somehow all she'd managed to do was push him away and now the baby was coming and Jack wasn't here.

Annaya phoned Natalie first and then her mother. It was only when her anxious friend came zooming around the corner in her banged-up little car to rush her to the hospital that she thought about calling Jack.

"You haven't called him?" Natalie said breathlessly, as the panicked driver swung around a bend and put her foot down to accelerate towards the hospital. "You better do it soon, Annaya, or he's going to miss the birth."

"Of course he's going to miss the birth!" Annaya replied, trying to keep the tears out of her voice. "He's all the way in Vegas and I'm in California. He'll never make it in time."

"Call him now."

It was hard to do anything now that her labor pains were in full force, but Natalie was focusing on getting them both to the hospital in one piece, so it was up to Annaya to force her shaking hands to pick up her cell and dial Jack's number. It was hard to speak through the waves of labor pain and her voice came in short, sharp bursts through her winces when she got through to Jack's voicemail.

"Jack!" she exclaimed irritably. "Where the hell are you? It's the ninth months of the pregnancy and you're not taking your calls? *I'm... having... the... baby!*"

Annaya hung up, fury and resentment making her feel even more hot and flustered than she already did and she gripped onto the car door handle as Natalie made another sharp turn. "Slow down, Natalie! You're going to kill us both."

"I am not delivering that baby."

It must have looked an absurd scene to anyone who might have been watching: two pregnant women zooming around the city towards the hospital, snapping and criticizing each other. But, as soon as Natalie pulled up at the hospital, she was nothing but supportive and went into full military mode in search of a nurse or doctor who would be able to take good care of Annaya and the baby.

Annaya gripped onto Natalie's hand tightly as the nurses wheeled her in a wheelchair towards the maternity ward, telling her to breathe, and she tried even harder not to cry. "He's not here..." she murmured to herself, "he's not here..."

Natalie gripped her shoulder firmly. "It's alright, Annaya. You're going to be OK. I'm here. Your Mum's on the way."

It was all of little comfort to Annaya. All she could think about was how she had left things with Jack and worry that because of her stupid big mouth, she'd have to do this on her own. She wanted to burst into tears and refuse to enter the ward until Jack was at her side, but she knew the baby wouldn't wait and so she gripped onto Natalie's hand for dear life and let the nurses whisk her away to the maternity ward. The baby was coming.

*****

Jack had been fuming ever since his argument with Annaya. How dare she accuse him of using her just for sex! At least, that's what he'd understood from the way she'd spoke about him flying in and out just to hook up. Of course whenever he saw Annaya he wanted to fall into bed with her, but that was because she was beautiful and smart and her eyes lit up when she saw him in a way that made Jack feel a million miles tall; powerful and wanted.

Everything about her drove him wild and whenever he was close to her he naturally wanted to tear off her clothes and press his lips down over hers, but that didn't mean that he was only after one thing.

The billionaire pondered all this sullenly in the days and weeks that passed after meeting Annaya's parents. Hadn't he done all he could to show Annaya that he cared? Hadn't he been there at the ultrasounds and weddings? Hadn't he called her faithfully every week? Hadn't he told her a hundred times that she did something to him? He'd treated her with a respect, patience and loyalty that he'd never shown any other woman, and she'd had the nerve to suggest that he was using her!

"You're reading too much into it," Lewis advised, as they sat together in front of an enormous flat screen TV in Jack's apartment one night.

"What do you mean?"

"She's pregnant. Hormones. Of course she's going to be all over the place. You're here; she's there. She probably feels abandoned or something. You know how women are."

"Not Annie. She's not like other women."

"Trust me, Jack; your Annie may be the best of the best in your eyes, but I've yet to meet a woman who doesn't get needy sometimes. You two have got this weird thing going on where you're going between screwing and planning how to raise a baby without ever really getting close to each other.

Women read into these things too much already, so how is something as complicated as what's going on between you and her not meant to drive her mad? She's pregnant with your child and probably has no idea whether you're around just for the baby or for her."

Jack was taken aback by Lewis' intuition and took a sip of an expensive beer with a pensive expression on his face. He hadn't quite thought of it in those terms before. He was happy to let the fire burn when he was in Annie's company, but perhaps for her it was all just a bunch of mixed messages for which he was to blame. Was she craving something more as much as he was?

"The whole thing is a nightmare," Jack said bitterly. "I don't know what the woman wants. I ask her to stay in Vegas and she's not interested. I propose, and she's not interested. What's a man meant to do to show a woman he's after more than sex? Tell me, Lewis, because I have no bloody idea."

The billionaire's friend laughed with amusement and gave Jack a knowing grin. "You're looking at the whole thing too logistically," he said wisely. "You're being too practical. Being physically close to her – together in Vegas or living in the same house -- isn't the same as being *close* to her."

"I'm not sure I'm following."

"Jesus, Jack, you're clueless. She wants you to commit to her *emotionally*. She wants you to show her that you care about *her* and that you aren't just sticking around for the sake of the baby or because of the press."

"How would you know?"

"Trust me, Jack. She wants you to wear your heart on your sleeve."

"I'm not sure how that's done."

"I know. You've slept with dozens of women, but I don't think I've ever seen you in love before. You're a mess."

"In love?"

"Jesus, Jack. Can't you tell?"

Jack fell silent and considered his friends words carefully. He knew that his feelings for Annaya were something stronger than those he'd had for women in the past. He knew that Annaya had been taking up a special place in his heart in the months that they'd got to know each other better, but he'd never really gone as far as to think of it as love.

He'd never been in love before, but perhaps that's what it was to be completely captivated by another person, to think about them first thing every morning and in the last moments of every night. Perhaps that's what it was to be driven mad by their mystery, but to still not consider for a moment walking away because you're just too damned into her.

"I've hardly spoken to her in weeks."

"She's the mother of your child. There's going to be a fair few more arguments yet, I'd imagine. You can't run away from them all."

"I'm not running away."

"Then pick up the phone and talk to her."

"Fine. I will."

Jack stood up and retreated into the kitchen to pull his cell phone out of his pocket and finally give in and tell Annaya that he was sorry for having given her the cold shoulder. When he pulled out his phone, however, he was shocked to find that he already had a missed call from her. He quickly entered his voicemail and his eyes widened and mouth quickly fell open when he heard Annaya's tense, short breaths down the line and her message to get there *as soon as possible*.

Lewis came into the kitchen to see what was taking so long when he didn't hear Jack speaking and then grew concerned when he saw Jack's face grow pale as he listened to his messages.

"What is it?"

"The baby's coming."

"Now?"

"*Now.*"

*****

The nurse wrapped up Annaya's little girl in a pink blanket and pressed her into her mother's arms. Annaya looked down at her newborn baby and felt an overwhelming surge of love and all the screaming and worry and pain of the last few hours washed away and was replaced by pure joy.

Her baby girl was beautiful: half Jack and half Annaya. She had light brown skin and hair that was dark and curly like Annaya's, but she had her father's nose and eyes. She was no bigger than a loaf of bread and the little cry she made as she looked around at the big wide world was the sweetest sound Annaya had ever heard.

She had just picked up her little girl for her first cuddle when a squeaking sound made her look up and she saw Jack come skidding around the doorway, his expensive shoes skidding on the lino. On seeing him, all her anger and fear vanished at once. Jack looked just as flustered and terrified as she had been just moments earlier, and his disheveled hair and crumpled suit told Annaya that he had come to be with her as quickly as possible. He didn't hate her, after all. She smiled at him and his eyes softened. He came to stand at her side.

Even now, with a baby in her arms, her thoughts were on what Jack would think of her in this state: pale and clammy with no make-up and her big belly pushing up the bed sheets, but Jack was completely captivated by the sight of their new child.

"My God..." he breathed disbelievingly. "She's beautiful."

"She's ours."

Jack stepped forward and hesitantly reached out a hand to gently brush his palm against his baby's head and then he let out a little half-breath of amazement and shook his head in awe again. "Incredible."

Suddenly, all of the emotion and upset of the day came flooding back and Annaya was struggling once more to hold back her tears. She finally ran out of strength to hold them back and a couple escaped over her eyelids. She looked up at Jack tearfully and said, "Jack, I'm sorry for everything."

"Ssh," Jack soothed her gently, laying a hand on her shoulder to press her back down when she tried to sit up to talk to him. "It's done. I'm sorry, too. I was mad, but I shouldn't have ignored you. I'm sorry that I wasn't here."

"You're here now."

Jack perched on the bed beside her and put an arm

around her shoulders. Finally, Annaya felt safe again and she let her head fall onto his shoulder and rest there for a while. She let a little fantasy grow in her mind's eye that this is how it would always be: her, Jack and the baby, snuggled close together, sharing a moment of complete peace and comfort.

*

Everything in Annaya's home was set up and ready for the baby. The little nursery she'd made out of a room that had been a disused home office was beautiful, painted in soft pinks with squishy little giraffes painted up the walls. The sweet little white pine crib was against one wall with a zoo-themed mobile full of soft little teddy bears hanging above and everything else that a baby could need was in the room with their daughter, whom they decided to name Alice.

The new mother couldn't wish for more for her little girl, who looked so perfect lying on top of her blankets, clutching a toy giraffe in her tiny little grasp, but Alice's father, who had been so overjoyed a few days before, began to grow more sullen and agitated in the days that followed, especially when he saw all the changes that had taken place in the nursery since he'd last visited Annaya.

"This room is a box, Annie."

"She's an infant, Jack. She hardly needs a palace."

"I don't understand why you won't just come back with me to Vegas."

Annaya gave him a patient but slightly stern look and reached out to stroke her baby's hair. She sighed. "No, you don't understand," she agreed. "My life is here, Jack. My job is here. My family is here. My best friend is here. You can't expect me to give all that up just to make things more convenient for you. It's going to be hard being a mother. I don't want to be on my own."

"That's precisely my point. Come to Vegas and you won't be on your own. You'll be with me."

"Surrounded by all those casinos?" Annaya pulled a face. "All that glitz and glam and high living is all well and fine for a girls night out, Jack, but it's hardly the right kind of environment to raise a child."

"You're being narrow-minded, Annie. There's more to Vegas than the nightlife. There are some good schools out there. I'd set you up somewhere away from the city, in a nice cozy little home, if that's what you wanted. I'd fly your family out whenever you wanted them around. Natalie, too. I'd do everything to make it work. I hate the thought of leaving you behind here."

Jack cast his gaze disdainfully around Annaya's little flat and she wondered if he was more upset to be leaving her, or to be leaving his daughter in a place that wasn't up to his standards. Of course, Annaya knew that she'd be provided for financially if she went with Jack, but it was everything else she needed that worried her. How would she feel out in another state, cooped up in some house he'd chosen for her with no friends or family around while he spent his days schmoozing with the big dogs?

Annaya looked over at Jack longingly. She loved that he wanted her and their daughter close. She loved that he'd do anything to have them with him. But she was always not naive enough to believe that everything would fall into place just because she was on his doorstep. They had rocky foundations and Annaya didn't want to let go of all her safety nets just yet.

"Let's see how it goes," she said reasonably.

"Whether or not we're together, we've got a daughter together now and that makes us a family. Family should stick together."

"I hear you, Jack. I'll think about it."

It was a torturous day that afternoon as the time grew nearer for Jack to return to Vegas and leave his new little family behind. He dragged his heels like a naughty schoolboy sent to the principal's office when he at last had to pick up his bags and head for the airport. Annaya tried to comfort him. She gave his hand a reassuring squeeze and looked up at him with sympathetic eyes.

"My doors are always open. You can come whenever you want."

"It's not the same. She's my daughter, too. I don't want her across state lines."

"I understand, Jack, but you can't expect me to just drop everything because it's what works best for you. My life is here and I won't leave that until a life with you seems secure."

Jack huffed angrily and clenched his jaw together to prevent him from saying something he'd regret. Eventually he let out a long sigh. "Why don't you trust me, Annie? Don't you think I'd take care of you?"

What was Annaya meant to say to that? She had no idea what kind of partner or father Jack would be. All their time had been spent together in short, intense bursts which Annaya knew were no reflection of real life. It was easy to be on your best behavior for a couple of days or a couple of weeks and a woman could forgive a handsome man anything when he was sweeping her off her feet and leading her to the bedroom.

Annaya had to keep telling herself that dreamy eyes and deep pockets were not the signs of a good partner. It took more than that, and she just didn't know for sure whether Jack would be the type to keep his cool when things got tough.

He went on and on about his responsibilities and

stepping up to his role in his father's company and how much pressure there was being in the public eye and meeting all his demands. How would he cope with a little one crying all hours of the night and wanting her Daddy's attention?

Annaya couldn't see Jack transforming into a family man overnight just because he'd felt awe at the sight of a newborn. What would he be like when the novelty wore off and he realized that she and Alice were there to stay? How soon would it be before he began to miss the casino lights and roulette wheels? How long before he started to miss the rush from getting his name in the papers for all the wrong reasons or falling into bed with a different woman every night?

Annaya knew the lifestyle Jack had come from and it

was fast-paced and glamorous. She just couldn't imagine that a simple life with her and Alice would satisfy him, and she knew for sure that hanging around in some big empty house on her own, waiting for him to come home and biting her tongue every time he flashed his bad reputation would not satisfy her.

She needed to see more of Jack in his role as a father and as he might be as a partner before she'd give everything up for him. She didn't want to be a phase in his life, when for her, he would be the center of her world.

"I trust you," she said softly, answering his question at last. "I just don't know what I want yet. I need time. The time we've spent together hasn't been real life."

"What do you mean?"

"It's been short bursts here and there. You hardly know me at all. Maybe I seem like someone exciting in a tight dress in a glamorous place, but normally I'm just a girl in a pair of jeans and a sweater, going about her dull, ordinary life. And now I'm a mother, too. I'm going to be breastfeeding and changing diapers and getting snappy because I haven't slept in days.

You're begging me to come over now, but neither of us know what we're going to be like when life is just ordinary. I want to see a bit of your ordinary before I leap into a life with you."

Jack sighed again and leaned against the doorframe with a sullen expression. "And what about me? I don't want to miss out on her." The billionaire crossed the flat to look over his daughter, sleeping soundly in her crib. His eyes grew soft as he watched over her. "I

294

don't want to leave her."

"Then don't," Annaya said simply. "My door is open. You can stay here as long as you want."

The billionaire let out a dry laugh. "It's not that easy."

"No? Well, it's not that easy for me, either."

"Let's not argue again, Annie. We have to get better at this. We've got Alice now. We can't resent each other."

Annaya knew he was right and she let out a little sigh. "I don't want you to leave, either."

"I'll come back next week," Jack vowed. "I'll come more often now that she's here. Just until we figure something out. Even if you don't want to be in Vegas all the time, maybe you could come for the summers or the holidays or *something*.

 I want a bit of ordinary, too. Not a short, sweet burst of excitement. Some long-term, dull and average with you and Alice. I'd like that a lot."

"Me, too. We'll figure it out, Jack. Some long-term, dull and average."

*****

It was almost unbearable being away from them. Ever since Alice had been born, Jack had been short-tempered, snappy and distracted and it was all because the only place he wanted to be was with his daughter and the woman who'd brought her into the world.

Annaya's words still stung him and he found it hard not to stew over them. She saw his suggestion that she come and stay in Vegas as a demand for her to leave everything behind, whereas he saw it as a way to be together. When he looked back over all their time together, he felt like he'd done everything right.

He'd made sure that Annie and the baby had everything they needed and he'd made sure to be there every step of the way. Of course, there was that stupid proposal which had come too soon and had been done in panic. No doubt, it made Annaya feel like he was after a wife for PR purposes, but the good intent had been there.

Now, somehow, he'd found himself further away from her than ever. It was bad enough being in separate states when it was just Annie that he was missing, but now that he was without his daughter too, Jack felt isolated and longing for the gentleness and comfort that only comes with family.

Matters in his own family were not running so smoothly. Jack's mother had died some years previously after battling an illness for a short time, which had left only him and his father to lock horns over public reputations and trust funds. Now, Brandon, too, was in poor health and deteriorating fast. It made it even more difficult for Jack to spend the time he wanted with Annaya and Alice, as his father grew less and less able to continue going at the same speed he had and Jack was required to step up and take the lead.

"It's good to see you stepping up, son," the tycoon told him over breakfast one morning.

Brandon had become so frail in recent months, ever since he'd had a stroke not long after Annaya had been introduced to him and turned down his proposal. His silver hair was not a definite and dull grey and his hands trembled so much that he no longer wrote his own signature, but turned everything over to Jack to process.

"You know how I've worried over what will come of my business when I'm not around, but you've been working hard lately to show me another side to yourself and I can tell you that it hasn't gone unnoticed. Does it have anything to do with Annaya, I wonder?"

Jack almost laughed from his surprise to hear his father be intuitive for once. It was unlike the old man to pick up on the subtler aspects of human emotion and Jack paused a moment before answering. "I just feel it's time to make a change," Jack told him with a nonchalant shrug. "I've had my time having fun and now it's time to step up. I have responsibilities now."

"Are you talking about the company or the granddaughter that I haven't met yet?"

"Both." Jack gave his father a sideways glance as he buttered a croissant. The tone in the old billionaire's voice suggested that he wanted to meet Alice, which surprised Jack. "I would've thought you wouldn't have wanted to see Annaya again, or the baby. Not after she turned down that proposal you were so keen on."

Brandon let out a husky cackle of laughter and took a sip of orange juice. He fixed his sharp, instinctive eyes on his son and smiled wisely. "I wanted *you* to settle down, son, but that woman had her head screwed on right. Truth be told, I admire her for not taking the easy path. It can't be easy for a woman facing single motherhood to turn down an offer like that."

"No," Jack agreed. "I still can't get my head around why she would."

"She's got her pride, and that's a good thing. It's nice to know that someone will keep an eye on you when I'm gone. Somebody with some common sense and a little bit of self-respect."

"You'll be around for a while yet."

"No, I won't, Jack, and we must be prepared for that. I want you to start shadowing Nathan a lot more closely and come to me with any questions. I've not got much time left to teach you all I know."

"I don't want to talk about things like that, father. It's morbid."

"It's practical. Let me tell you something that I learned the hard way: you have to be a realist. Things aren't always going to go your way. People won't always do what you want them to do. Yet, you always have to find a way somehow to come out on top. You have to plan for the worst and be prepared. I'm not going to be around much longer, Jack. That's a fact. Soon, everything will be handed over to you and I'm trusting that you'll be up to the task."

"I've been trying to show you that I can handle it."

"Yes, and you've impressed. I think that woman has made you get your priorities in order. I'd like to see her again before I go, and meet my granddaughter, too."

"I've been trying to avoid the publicity, father. I know how you hate a PR storm."

"It's rarely that I put anything before my company's good reputation, but there are extraordinary measures occasionally, even for me. I'd like to meet them both here, Jack. Will you arrange that for me?"

"I'll put it forward to Annaya."

"Good, good."

The two men sat back and both continued with their breakfasts. Jack felt all his responsibilities weighing heavily on his shoulders. It was getting more and more difficult to split his time between Vegas and California and his father's expectations of him were growing greater. Now he wanted to bring Annaya and Alice into the mix, and Jack wondered if that wouldn't end up being just the kind of tense situation that Annaya believed he couldn't handle. Well, they'd just have to wait and see.

*****

"So, are you going to go?"

"I don't know, Natalie. Do you think I should?"

Whenever things between Annaya and Jack became too confusing or hard to decipher, Natalie was always there to give Annaya a push in one direction or the other. The two women were sitting together on the patio of a little coffee shop. Alice was in her pram, half-asleep and just occasionally letting her dozy eyes flutter open to look up at the slightly cloudy sky. Annaya rocked her back and forth as she went through this new dilemma with her best friend, who was also getting close to her due date.

"Of course you should, Annaya. I don't get why you're always so hesitant when it comes to Jack. It's obvious that you're mad about him."

"Well, he's every woman's dream, isn't he?" Annaya agreed. "But that's why he's dangerous. It would be so easy to confuse admiration for love, and I don't want to fall into that trap. I don't want to find myself stranded in Vegas with a baby just because I couldn't see past the stars in my eyes."

"You're such a cynic!" Natalie half-laughed. "Why are you holding back from him? It seems to me like he's really making an effort to show you that he wants to be there for you and Alice."

"I know he does, but the question is *in what way* does he want to be there for us?" Annaya sighed heavily and stirred her coffee absent-mindedly. "I guess I'm just worried that he's in this honeymoon phase and reality hasn't struck him yet. I mean, look at his life and the women he's had. How long until he gets bored of me and Alice? And what will I do if he tries to shrug us off?"

"Do you think he will?"

"I just don't know."

"I think you're being paranoid. Take a risk Annie, for once in your life, and I don't mean skinny-dipping or skydiving or any other of those 'risks' you're so proud of. I'm talking about actually doing something that scares you. Stepping into a situation when you know you've got something to lose. You've been the same forever. You never give guys a fair chance."

"That's not true. I just don't waste my time when I know it's not right. When you know, you know, right?"

"And what about Jack? Do you *know*?"

Annaya sighed again. She thought she knew. Then again, thinking she knew wasn't the same as *knowing* she knew. What did she actually know? Only that she trembled when he was near her and that she missed him every day that he was gone. She avoided the question and its difficult answer.

"What was it like with Daniel?"

"I knew," Natalie chuckled. "It was just the way he made me feel."

"Like?"

"Like I was beautiful and smart and wanted. Butterflies. Mad about him. I don't know, Annaya. It was just all those things you read about in romance novels. Fireworks, and all the rest. I went weak at the knees every time I saw him and wanted to spend every second of every day with him. I was more scared of losing him than any other guy I'd ever been with."

Everything Natalie said rang true for Annaya. Jack made her feel all those things and more, and the thought of the handsome billionaire finding a younger, more adventurous or more glamorous woman to replace her made her stomach clench in fear. She never wanted to be without him. Why was she holding back?

In reality, she knew why. It was because right now, while their relationship was undefined, nothing was on the line. She still had the choice to dive right in or pull away without doing too much damage. Yet, if she *did* choose to dive in and put everything into her and Jack, then she created the possibility that she could lose it all.

If they found that, once together, they got under each other's feet, or argued all the time, or had problems, then she'd risk losing what they had right now; as lukewarm and difficult to understand as it was. She could lose him altogether to resentment or anger or nostalgia, and Annaya just didn't want that to happen.

"You have to take a leap of faith sometime, Annaya," Natalie advised kindly. "Besides, this would just be a visit, right? Go out there for a few weeks and see how you feel."

"You're right. I'll go there. Meet his father again. See what Vegas is like with a newborn. See what Jack is like with a family. God, Natalie, the whole thing terrifies me."

"That's a good thing," Natalie laughed. "It means it's something you really want to work out. I've got my fingers crossed for you, Annaya. I hope it does work out. He's just like Prince Charming."

Chapter10

Annaya cringed as she stepped into the foyer. The last time she'd been here, Jack had proposed to her. The memory of him down on one knee for all the wrong reasons still made her feel embarrassed, but at least now she could look back on it and laugh, knowing that he'd done it out of panic and noble intentions. She looked up at the tall ceilings and those chandeliers and marveled again at just how much she'd turned down when she'd said no.

This time, she wasn't alone when she stepped into the mansion. Jack had come all the way to California to help her fly out with Alice and all her baby things and they arrived together at the Casali Estate, which still took Annaya's breath away, although Jack navigated his way around the palatial home with aristocratic ease.

It was remarkable how comfortable he was in these surroundings and Annaya had to admit that there was something very attractive about a man so comfortable in luxury. It gave Jack an air of sophistication and power that was very appealing, although Annaya knew him well enough by now to know that there was always more than what was on the surface.

She wouldn't be staying at Jack's place this time, but in the mansion itself with Jack's father, Alice's grandfather. The thought made Annaya's mind boggle. Although she and Jack were not anything defined right now and she had no right to any of this extravagance, her daughter was related to all of it by blood. Her grandfather was the billionaire who had commissioned this glorious building and brought in millions of dollars month after month. Her father was the one who would take it all after Brandon died.

Yes, Annaya's little girl had an incredible life ahead of her and it made Annaya's head spin to wonder at how she was going to manage to raise a daughter with a foot in both worlds. How would little Alice ever appreciate her mother's home-cooked meals and pot plants when there was a swimming pool and horses at Daddy's house? It made Annaya uncomfortable to think that she'd ever had to compete with Jack for her daughter's affections, but they were the sort of worries that came to the surface when surrounded by such incredible wealth.

Annaya picked up her daughter from her pram and

cradled her closely to her chest. Thank God she was still so small and innocent and too young to care for diamonds. Thank God that she was still just a baby who wanted nothing more than her stuffed giraffe to keep her happy and an occasional hug from Mummy.

"Should I take her for a while?" Jack offered.

The new mother had been incredibly protective of her daughter throughout the flight. Annaya hadn't like the way that the poor little baby had howled at the discomfort of the plane's altitude and had felt wary of everyone else in the lines at security, as though strangers wanted to do her daughter harm. Annaya was a lioness when it came to her baby girl and she hadn't even relinquished Alice to Jack on the journey. Now her father was holding out his arms expectantly, wanting to help and have his own chance to be close to his child.

Annaya smiled and gently passed the little bundle over. Jack's eyes still lit up in awe every time he caught sight of his little girl and his strong, powerful arms became a cradle for her when he held his baby. The second he took Alice into his arms, his polished, playboy billionaire exterior dropped off like an old coat, and beneath it was a natural father and family man. Annaya still wasn't sure which was the real Jack, or how long this family man would remain.

"She loves her daddy," she said softly, smiling at the sight of Jack cuddling his daughter.

"Daddy loves her. I know who else is going to love her, too. It's time for Alice to meet my father."

It made the guest nervous to know that she would be

coming face-to-face with Brandon again. She still wasn't sure how she felt about the man. He'd been so hospitable and welcoming when she'd last been here, but then she'd come to find that he'd been manipulating the situation the whole time, trying to nudge her into an engagement with his son.

She had no idea how he would feel about her now that she'd said no. She wanted to hold onto Jack's hand for comfort as they headed towards the sitting room to meet him, but the father of her child had his arms full with Alice, so Annaya had no choice but to let her own hands fall loosely at her sides and to bite down nervously on her lip, awaiting her second introduction to the original Casali billionaire.

Brandon was waiting for them in the sitting room and he was not as Annaya remembered. The last time she'd seen him, he'd been a picture of health and brute force: a large and sturdy presence, with a steady stance and broad shoulders. Now he seemed like a shadow of that man: weak, shaky and hunched over. He'd aged a hundred years since she'd last seen him and was sitting in a wicker chair by the window with a blanket over his now thin legs. She looked up at Jack questioningly and he lowered his voice to explain to her.

"He's not in good health."

"I know that, but I didn't expect..."

"I know."

Annaya suddenly felt a surge of sympathy for Jack. She'd always taken her own family for granted, but she could understand now why Jack was so keen to have her and Alice around. It was bad enough to be on your own in life, but how much lonelier must it feel to be on your own and rattling around in a place as big as this?

Surely it must have been weighing on Jack's mind that soon his father would be gone and then he'd be in Vegas all in his own in palaces not built for one. She laid a hand on the back of his arm comfortingly and he seemed surprised at her touch, which was the most tender she'd offered in a while. He smiled at her gratefully and then carried his daughter over to his father.

"Dad, this is my daughter, Alice, and you remember Annaya."

"How could I forget? A pleasure to see you again, my dear."

"Nice to see you, Brandon."

They greeted each other like they were old friends,
even though the last time they had met had been a
strange occasion, which had ended in an even more
bizarre twist. It seemed that they'd all chosen to put
all that behind them now and they sat together around
a low, ornate coffee table. They had a conversation
that could have been had between any man and his
son and daughter-in-law on any ordinary day. Annaya
wasn't sure how to react to such a familiar greeting,
but she decided to smile and act like this was the most
normal thing in the world: just her, her billionaire
lover and his dying father, and her newborn daughter,
who would be heiress to it all.

*

Jack's duties hadn't stopped just because Annaya was

visiting and while she and Alice were at home with his father, it was down to him to get on with business. That was how he'd found himself at the country club on a Wednesday afternoon to meet with a shareholder. The meeting went well, but it was after the shareholder had left that the trouble started.

The billionaire's ex, Hannah, was there again and Jack rolled his eyes. It didn't surprise him that the gold-digging woman had nowhere else to be in the middle of the day than to hang around the country club in the hopes of attracting the attention of a handsome man. She spotted Jack from a mile away and the petite blonde slithered across the lobby to sidle up to him.

"Jack!" she cooed. "Darling, it's good to see you. I wanted to apologize for my awful behavior last week.

I'd had a difficult couple of weeks, what with mother going through her divorce and everything and, well, I suppose I took it out on you. Will you forgive me?"

"Forget about it."

Jack didn't have time for Hannah and her antics. At home he had a beautiful woman waiting for him who had come all the way from Bakersfield to spend time with his father and he didn't want to be away from her for a second longer than necessary.

"I heard about your father taking a turn for the worse. I'm sorry for the sad news, Jack."

Here it was. Her real motive. Women like Hannah, who were raised to be the wives of rich men, could sniff out an inheritance like bloodhounds. Jack could sense the gold-digger preparing to pounce on him and his impending fortune and he tried to conceal a scowl. This was precisely the reason he cared for Annaya so much. The woman he had at home had far too much self-respect to ever throw herself at a man just because he had an impressive bank account. Her feelings were rooted in sincerity and not switched on and off again at the prospect of rich living.

"He's really not all that bad, Hannah. No reason to worry yourself."

"Oh, really? I'd heard he'd had a stroke."

"News travels fast around here."

"It's a concern, Jack. We care about your father and, of course, you. You know, if you ever wanted to talk about it, I'd be happy to lend an ear. I know it must be tough now that your mother's gone..."

Her tactics were blatant and it made Jack's skin crawl. There wasn't any genuineness or integrity in the woman at all. He couldn't believe that he'd wasted time on women like Hannah when there were women like Annaya in the world.

"I'm fine. Really."

"What about that baby that was on the way? How has that all turned out?"

"Again, there's no need for you to worry about it."

"I heard that there's a woman staying at your father's house. Is that her?"

"What is this, Hannah? Are you having us followed?"

The blonde let out a light little laugh that sounded more like a cackle to Jack's ears and he frowned.

"Followed, Jack? Don't be so dramatic! Of course not. You know how word travels in small circles. The gardener probably told someone, or the maid. Word got around to my mother. I heard it from her."

"Well, ignore the gossip. It's not true."

Jack felt guilty to be lying about Annaya's presence in the mansion and denying that she was around, but he was doing it for her own protection as well as his own. Neither of them needed a flock of journalists around them right now and it was simply better for all concerned if their private lives could stay private, especially around opportunists like Hannah.

"Isn't it? If I was your girl, Jack, I wouldn't want you to be keeping me behind closed doors."

"It's not like that."

"No? You're keeping her quite the secret."

"Yes. Yet, it got out into the press somehow, didn't it?"

"That story that was in the magazines? Yes! Shocking, isn't it? I read about it. Those journalists are vultures, aren't they?"

Hannah's face was revealing nothing, but Jack knew damned well that she was behind the story being leaked and he hated that he had to be on his best behavior in this country club for the sake of his reputation rather than putting the conniving woman in her place with a few home truths.

He sighed heavily. "I'm done here. Nice seeing you again."

"You too, Jack. You know, you should bring that

mystery woman of yours here sometime. We're all dying to meet her."

"Perhaps."

Jack left the club feeling unsettled. He was sure that Hannah had something on her mind, although he had no idea what it was. Undoubtedly, she was aware that very soon Jack would inherit everything and she wanted to get as close to him as possible for when his ship came in. It sickened him to think that there were women in the world with those kind of motives when an old man was dying, but at least he had Annaya to vent to when he got in again.

"She was practically dancing on his grave already, Annie!" he fumed when he'd returned to the mansion later that evening and the two were putting Alice to bed together. "All she wants is to stick her nose in now that he's on his deathbed to try and get in on his fortune. It's disgusting."

"I can't believe anyone can behave like that," Annaya agreed, laying Alice down. "I hope you told her where to go."

"Of course I did. I have no interest in women like that. She wanted me to bring you into the club. Heavens knows why. She's plotting something."

"Oh, don't worry, Jack. I wouldn't blow your cover like that."

Annaya said it in a voice that was crossed between amusement and disdain and she raised her eyebrows at him in slight irritation. Jack knew why. Ever since she'd come to visit him in Vegas, he'd practically kept her under house arrest out of fear that her name and face would end up in the papers and throw her life into the spotlight. He saw it as protecting her, but he knew that she felt like he was ashamed of her. He laid a hand comfortingly on her shoulder.

"It's not about blowing my cover, Annie. It's about stopping the vultures from swarming all over you. Once they've got your name, they won't leave you alone. They'll follow you everywhere with cameras and microphones in your face, and Alice, too. Do you really want photographers crowding around our baby? I don't want her to be exposed to all that."

"You're right," Annie sighed, looking down tenderly at the face of her innocent newborn. "It's just, something's got to give eventually, Jack. You can't hide her forever... or me."

"I'm not hiding anything," Jack insisted again. "I'm

protecting you. You know that I have nothing but respect for you. I'm proud that you're the mother of my child. Seeing Hannah again just drove it all home. You're miles above all the women I've ever known, Annie. You're special to me."

The billionaire caught her eyes earnestly and he could almost see Annaya's heart flutter. Her eyes widened with emotion when he said those words to her. But she was too strong to be swayed by sweet nothings and she took a short, sharp breath and busied herself with folding Alice's tiny little romper suits.

"Yes, well, all those things will sort themselves out in the end. You just need to decide how and when you're going to 'present' us, if that's what needs doing. It can be done in your own time, Jack, but it has to be done eventually. It's a very nice mansion, but I don't particularly enjoy being cooped up all the time, no matter how grand it all is."

*****

Annaya wouldn't let it show how hurt she felt every time that Jack shunned her and Alice whenever there was a chance that the wrong people would see their faces. She knew that he believed he was protecting them, but she was also convinced that there was a little shame there, also. After all, she was from a completely different world to him. In comparison to Jack she was dull, uneducated and common. For now, she was prepared to stay out of the limelight and look after Alice behind closed doors, but she couldn't see a future with Jack in which she never stepped outside unless a chauffeur dropped her off miles away from the Casali family.

"How did the meeting go today, son?"

Brandon, Jack and Annaya were eating together. It was fairly late, as Jack had had other meetings after his one in the country club and then the two new parents had put their daughter to bed before settling down for dinner. Now the dying billionaire was keen to hear what his son had been doing with himself all day.

"It went well," Jack nodded. "All the shareholders are happy with the proposals for the new developments and the profit we're turning. No problems at all."

"Good, good. That's what I like to hear." Brandon turned his attention towards Annaya to tell her more about what Jack was doing in the company. "When I go, which won't be long now, I'm afraid, Jack will be in charge of all of this." The billionaire gestured around the mansion proudly. "He's my only son. All of this will be his and then Alice's in time."

"It's a big responsibility," Annaya said carefully. She was impressed Jack was able to manage all of this grandeur and enterprise, but she wasn't sure that she ever wanted all that pressure to fall on her daughter's shoulders. What if Alice wanted to be a painter or a dancer? Annaya wouldn't want her to feel like she was bound by the duties of the Casali name, which was the one on her birth certificate.

"Oh yes," Brandon nodded, his chest puffing up proudly. "$2.3 billion of responsibility, to be precise. At first, I was worried Jack wouldn't rise to the challenge, but he's proved me wrong. I think meeting you has done him good. He's a father now."

Annaya smiled. It still felt strange to hear anybody

say that out loud. She was a mother and that gorgeous man sitting across the table from her was the father.

"Being a father changes a man," Brandon said wisely. "You wouldn't believe it now, but I was once very much like Jack – wild and reckless. Although, I didn't have the status or financial freedom that Jack has now. It's harmless being a reckless youth when nobody knows who you are. In truth, I respect how difficult it has been for Jack growing up the way he has. There's a lot of pressure being a Casali. Luckily, Alice will have a mother to give her a break from all of this. You have family in California, don't you? Parents? Siblings?"

"Parents, yes. A sister."

"That's good; somewhere for my granddaughter to escape to once in a while. I wish Jack had had the

333

same."

Annaya smiled again and looked over to Jack who was half-smiling himself to hear his father talking about his childhood. Annaya had the feeling that he didn't hear his father reminisce all that often. She was glad that Brandon had given his blessing for Alice to spend her fair share of time in the real world with Annaya and her family. Annaya would never deny her all the love and comfort of regular family life, which she wasn't sure she'd ever experience in a place as formal and expansive as this one.

After dinner, she went to check on her daughter, Jack was only a few steps behind.

"You were quiet over dinner."

"Was I?"

"Yes. Is there something wrong?"

"No, Jack. Everything's fine." Annaya looked down at Alice, who was sleeping soundly, feeling right at home, even if Annie didn't and she sighed. She turned to look at Jack with her arms folded self-consciously across her chest and she looked up at him uncertainly. "Is this ever going to work?"

"What do you mean?"

"We're so different."

"Are we?"

Annaya laughed scornfully and gestured around the impressive and grand nursery that made Alice's room back home look like a scruffy shoebox. "Aren't we?"

"It's just money, Annie. I don't think we're that

335

different at all." Jack stepped across to the anxious woman and held her shoulders, encouraging her to look up into his earnest eyes. "You are strong and determined and can stand on your own two feet. I like to think that I can do the same. You're vibrant and sexy and adventurous, and I'm no wallflower either. We're a lot alike."

"You're just saying that. Wouldn't you much rather have gotten a woman pregnant who would give a better impression to the press? Some private school sorority girl with rich parents?"

"Do you think I'm that shallow?"

Annaya sighed. "I don't know how I feel, Jack. Most new fathers don't hide their daughters from the world at all costs. She's not some dirty little secret, you know."

"I know that," Jack said, and Annaya could hear the hurt in his voice. "She's my world now. I'd do anything for her."

"I want you to stop worrying about the press," Annie urged gently. "I want us to spend time together without always looking over our shoulders. Some normal family time."

"Alright," Jack conceded after a brief pause and a sigh. He shrugged and his hand reached up to brush back a strand of hair tenderly from Annie's eyes. "If that's what you want. But know that you're in for a lot of attention."

Annie smiled. "We can handle it."

The Final Chapter

The country club was as luxurious as Brandon's mansion and even more full of the elite. Everywhere Annaya looked, she spotted another person who looked like they'd crawled out the pages of some glossy magazine. They were holding tennis racquets and golf clubs, but none of them looked like they'd been putting that much effort into athletic pursuits. They were all immaculately dressed in cashmere and silk and Annaya self-consciously smoothed down the material of the ludicrously expensive navy pencil skirt and white chiffon blouse that Jack had suggested she wear.

She'd felt nervous the second he'd held out an outfit

for her, realizing that the clothes in her suitcase weren't good enough for his circles, but she'd swallowed back her disdain because she knew that Jack was introducing her to his circles for her sake, even though it might make life difficult for him.

In the club, Jack didn't hold her hand, but he did steer her by the shoulder through the lobby and into a bar that looked more like a library, with ornate carved chairs and elaborately upholstered furniture. Annaya could feel all eyes on her as she walked through the club, both because she was an unfamiliar face and because she was with Jack Casali. It wasn't long before the members of the club began to swarm.

"Jack! Long time, no see," one middle-aged man with a rotund stomach and a navy jacket exclaimed loudly. "And who is this lovely young woman?"

"This is Annaya Towler," Jack introduced her formally. "She's a family friend and staying with my father for a few weeks."

"Miss Towler, it's a pleasure."

The small talk lasted a few minutes and then the next nosy club member came along and then the next. Each time Jack introduced Annaya as a friend and it made her grow angrier and angrier, until by the time she came to leave, she was fuming and practically stormed towards the car that the valet had brought round, barely able to hold back her temper. Jack held open the door for her and she furiously climbed in. The billionaire climbed in besides her and gave her a questioning look.

"What's wrong with you?" he asked innocently.

"What's wrong with me?" Annaya seethed.

She couldn't believe that he was that clueless. She'd left her child at home for this and all Jack had done was introduce her as a friend. She'd been so touched and impressed that he'd been willing to finally present her to his world and claim her and Alice as his own in front of all his acquaintances, but all he'd done was save his own skin by creating a cover story for her presence at the mansion. Is that was why Alice was at the mansion? So that there'd be no questions about the baby? Is that why she was wearing such a tight skirt? So that it would hold in the last of her baby stomach? The tears prickled behind her eyes. She was so disappointed in him and embarrassed at herself for imagining a scenario in which he proudly presented her to the world.

"Forget it, Jack. It's not worth explaining."

She folded her arms defiantly over her chest and stared out the window with a clenched jaw, unwilling to let Jack see her cry. She told herself that she'd been the one to turn down a proposal and that she'd been the one to turn down his kisses and that she had no right to expect anything more from him now. They weren't a couple. They weren't an item. They were two completely different people who'd just happened to have a baby together.

She couldn't wait to get back to the mansion to pack and go home. She'd had enough of being here, where she was nothing but Jack's secret. She wasn't willing to be the person he vented to when he was angry or came to when he needed a break from his fast-paced corporate world.

And then, the one that he ignored when people were looking. She had more self-respect that that. She deserved better. Screw his fancy cars and mansions. Annaya didn't need any of it. She and her daughter were going home, where people loved them for who they were and would never try to hide them.

As soon as she was back at the mansion she stormed into the baby's room and began throwing Alice's things into a case. Jack quickly caught up with her and watched in amazement as she packed. "Annie, *talk* to me," he insisted. "What is going on?"

Annaya spun on her heel with hot, furious tears in her eyes and stood her ground, lifting her chin defiantly in the presence of the billionaire. "You were meant to introduce me to people tonight, Jack," she seethed, "but all you did was call me 'a family friend'. You didn't mention Alice at all. You're ashamed of us and you don't really want us here. Well, I've come here for your father's sake and he's met his granddaughter. Now I'm going home."

"Annie, you can't do that."

Jack went to take hold of her arm to stop her furious packing but she tore it away. "I can do whatever the hell I want, Jack. I'm not somebody you can buy."

"*Enough*!" Jack snapped, his own anger beginning to flare. "Enough of you insinuating that I'm shallow and conceited and ashamed of you and my daughter. I am not a bad man, Annie, and I'm mad about you."

His anger quickly melted into his passion and it was the two combined that compelled him to step across the room and press his lips down over Annaya's. All

Annie's fury melted away when she felt his mouth against her lips and she let all her anger out in a low moan. All that repressed sexual tension and love for him had only helped to fuel her anger. It was bad enough feeling like he was ignoring her, but that resentment was made so much worse when she was crazy for him. Now he was kissing her and it was very clear that her passions were not unreturned. She curled her fingers around his collar and led him down the corridor into her own guest room, away from Alice, where they could be alone.

"What are we doing, Jack?" she muttered between kisses, even as her fingers frantically unbuttoned his shirt. "What are we doing?"

"Ssh..." Jack urged her. "Let's not over-think it. It feels right."

"It feels right..." Annaya repeated dreamily. It felt *so* right. It felt right when his fingers ran through her hair and when his lips pressed down over her mouth and her neck and her shoulders. It felt right when he tore her shirt off her body and ripped off her bra. It felt right when he sucked and bit down on her nipples and when he threw her down on the bed. It felt right when he parted her legs and when he finally entered her.

Gasping and moving her hips against his, they made love again, for the first time since Alice had been born. If anything, it felt even more intense now that they had a daughter to make the bond between them even deeper and even more special. Annaya relished every second of him inside her and their bodies moving together. This was the way it was meant to be, she knew. This was what she wanted.

*****

"This time will be different," Jack promised her. "It's the gala of the year. Anybody who is anybody will be there and I will proudly tell every single one of those boring bastards that you are the mother of my child."

Annaya smiled and prayed that it was true. She was dressed in the most phenomenal dress that she would ever wear in her life: a floor length black gown with lace details around the shoulders and a sweetheart neckline which emphasized her breasts in a subtle, but devastating way.

She looked incredible and with her hair expertly styled on the top of her head and a sensational diamond necklace borrowed from the jewelry box of Jack's late mother.

Annaya knew that she had no reason to feel self-conscious. She looked and felt a million dollars, and she could see in Jack's eyes when he looked at her that he thought so, too. He kept finding reasons to put his hands on her shoulders or to brush back her hair as though he couldn't keep his hands off her and the memories of the night before were amazing, but confusing.

Even now, Jack was telling her that he would introduce her as Alice's mother – was that all? What did he think of her as a woman? Was there a future for them together as anything other than Alice's parents? The spark between them was only growing stronger and Annaya was hoping that an introduction to his friends and colleagues would be the final step towards breaking the final barriers and allowing them to think about a future together.

There was still a long way to go, of course, and so many things to consider. Annaya still didn't want to be away from her own parents in California, or away from Natalie, but the longer she spent at Brandon's mansion, the less uncomfortable she felt surrounded by such grandeur and the more it felt normal to her and she could imagine herself being here.

Perhaps Alice wouldn't grow up spoilt, even if her home was incredible beyond belief and her daddy a billionaire. Perhaps there was some way to make the two worlds merge in Vegas, after all, and Annaya could somehow find a way to give both the best of her and Jack to their daughter.

She worried about Jack. He was a strong man and not one to get too emotional, but she could see the strain that his father's ill health was having on him. It was partially the pressures of his new work demands that were making him seem so tired, but she was sure that it was also the knowledge that soon his father would be gone.

 No matter how distant from each other they'd been over the years, or in what ways they weren't close, they were still father and son, and when Brandon died, Jack would have nobody left.

"I can't believe that you manage to handle all you do, Jack," Annaya said softly, running her hands over his shoulders to smooth out his jacket. She felt herself tingle at the sensation of those strong, broad shoulders under her fingertips. "I'm sorry that I've been so demanding. I didn't realize quite how much you were dealing with."

Jack smiled at her, like he was seeing something that

nobody else saw, but that was only because Annaya was seeing something in him that others didn't perceive; the weight of the world on his shoulders. He kissed her forehead tenderly, but didn't let it turn into anything more than that. He was trying to resist her until he could figure out what the hell he was doing.

"You've nothing to be sorry for, Annie. I wish I could have been there more. I'm just glad you're here now. It's nice to have you around. And tonight, we'll have an incredible evening together. The press will snap us, people will talk and we won't give a damn."

"It sounds wonderful."

Jack's warnings hadn't gone unheard. Annaya knew that being photographed at the gala with Jack would open the door into a whirlwind of press attention, but she was ready to put herself in the spotlight in order to bring her daughter out of the shadows.

She didn't want Alice to grow up feeling shunned by her daddy or ashamed of her mother. Annaya and Jack needed to present a united front to the world and be on the same page in order for Alice to have the best. That was what tonight was about, even though seeing Jack in his black suit, looking as suave and sexy as the first night she'd met him, made Annaya feel much more like the night was a night for them.

Alice was being taken care of by the mansion's staff and although Annaya hated it every time she left her little girl behind, she was looking forward to a night of dancing and time spent with Jack. They climbed into a waiting limousine together and Annie felt her stomach doing little nervous flips during the drive.

Finally, they pulled up outside the casino where she

and Jack had met for the first time and even before she'd stepped out of the car she could see the lights flashing outside. The press were here. The car pulled up at the entrance of the casino and she and Jack looked at each other for one last moment of privacy.

"Are you ready for this?" Jack asked her earnestly. "There's no turning back."

"I'm ready."

A man in a smart suit opened the limousine door and Annaya stepped out. The camera lights made spots dance in front of her eyes and she felt almost overwhelmed by the attention the event was earning from the press and the attention that she was earning now that she'd stepped out of a limousine; attention which only increased when Jack stepped out behind her.

She began to wonder if she'd made a mistake and thought that maybe Jack had been right all along, but then he took her hand all her fears melted away. Tonight she was not here as his secret, but as his date, and she felt like a princess holding onto his arm. A big smile jumped to her face and she looked up at Jack with adoring eyes as the camera flashed. She had no doubts left. None at all.

*****

Jack was filled with pride when the photographers surrounded them. He'd been worried that Annaya would be overwhelmed by the attention, but just like everything that came Annaya's way, she dealt with it with grace and dignity, smiling for the cameras without playing up to them and squeezing Jack's hand for reassurance without pressing up against him in a way that would allow people to make assumptions before they'd spoken for themselves. The questions came soon enough.

"Mr. Casali! Who is your date tonight?"

"This is Miss Annaya Towler. She's the mother of my beautiful daughter, Alice."

"Was it a planned child, Mr. Casali?"

Jack laughed lightly. "I wouldn't change a thing."

"What is the nature of yours and Miss Towler's relationship, Mr. Casali?"

"She is an incredible woman that I'm proud to have as my date tonight."

"Do we hear wedding bells, Mr Casali?"

"Perhaps one day. For now we're enjoying being new parents."

"How did you meet?"

This time the microphone was directed at Annaya and for a moment she was afraid she wouldn't be able to get any words out at all, but then she found her voice and smiled, looking up at Jack to follow his confident lead.

"We met at this very casino, in fact. I was celebrating an engagement with my closest friend and Jack was working in the casino. I guess you could say we clicked."

"How long have you been an item?"

"Our relationship has been growing stronger for almost a year now."

Talking to the press was an art. It was all about giving answers without giving the full details. Annaya was beginning to understand Jack's tendency to skirt around the details when dealing with the press. It was an uncomfortable feeling to know that these people could find out anything about you and spin it into a story. It felt like good practice to keep some things close to your chest in order to feel like some things were still private.

It was especially hard to know what to say when asked to answer questions about the nature of their relationship when neither were really sure themselves. Annaya, fortunately, was a natural at dodging difficult questions with grace.

"You must feel very lucky, Miss Towler. Mr Casali is a catch."

"Yes, he is, and I do. I feel very fortunate that he's Alice's father. She's a very lucky girl."

The questions ranged from pushing for details about their relationship to questions about Alice and their plans for the future. It did become tiring after a while and a little overwhelming, but Annaya held her own and whenever a question was a little too complex, she only had to look up at Jack for the billionaire to take the lead. They were a natural celebrity couple, supporting each other as the vultures gathered around them.

Finally, they were able to tear themselves away from the photographers and head inside to where the gala was taking place. It was an opulent affair with women dripping in diamonds and men sipping champagne, but for once, Annaya wasn't intimidated by the grandeur of it all. The last week and a half with the Casalis had made her feel more at ease among the finer things, and she held her head up high as though she belonged there.

She moved from group to group with Jack at her side, being introduced and engaging in small talk with a smile and light laugh and didn't feel self-conscious or insecure at all until a stunning blonde came their way.

She was a slim woman, with a large chest and shapely legs, wearing the most stunning grey silk dress that emanated class and sophistication. She had naturally radiant blonde hair that had been styled into classic waves for the occasion and she wore a dash of red lipstick across her lips.

The entire effect made her look like a movie star from the forties and even Annaya's eyes widened at the sight of such a beauty coming their way. The woman had a predatory smile and narrow eyes.

Annaya had no idea who she was, but the woman seemed to recognize her. The stranger glided across the casino towards them and came to a stop in front of Jack, resting her weight and a hand on one hip so that each of her womanly curves were emphasized.

"Jack. It's good to see you. I wasn't sure you'd make it."

The beautiful blonde flicked her gaze up and down over Annaya's body and her eyebrows lifted in an expression that showed she was unimpressed. Suddenly Annaya felt like the diamonds and ball gown couldn't hide who she really was and she felt her cheeks flush under the stunning woman's judgmental gaze.

"Hannah." Jack greeted dryly. His voice was cold and stern, but Jack's ex was not deterred. She turned her attention sharply to Annaya.

"Is this the woman you've been hiding?"

"I've not been hiding anybody."

"Oh really? Because last time we met you told me to ignore the gossip. You said that none of it was true."

"You know better than anybody just how hard it is to keep your private lives away from the press, Hannah. I've been protecting a woman who means a lot to me."

"Then it's time for the grand reveal. Tell me all about her."

Annaya didn't like the way that Hannah spoke about her rather than to her, addressing Jack directly as if

Annaya wasn't there. She took an instant dislike to Jack's ex and tried to hide her scowl by taking a sip of her champagne and stepping slightly closer to Jack.

"This is Annaya. She's the mother of our daughter."

"So it *is* true. You're a father now. Congratulations."

The conniving blonde said the words, but she didn't sound pleased for them in the slightest. Annaya could hear the envy seeping through her words and when Jack was whisked away by a shareholder, Annaya was horrified to be left alone with the spiteful woman.

"You must be really pleased with yourself," Hannah said hostilely when Jack was out of earshot. She took a short, sharp gulp of her champagne and flashed a scowl at Annaya. It made her beautiful face instantly ugly.

"I'm sorry?"

"Really, getting pregnant? That's so vulgar. It's the most common means of tying down a man. A woman from his own social circles would never stoop to such lows."

"No?" Annaya replied, equally cold. "She'd just leak a story to the press?"

A cruel smile crossed Hannah's lips and she let out a low laugh. "He was mine long before he was yours, Annaya. You're just a novelty to him. He likes the idea of being a family man now, while his father's on his deathbed and he's facing life in that big old mansion alone, but it won't be long before the loneliness passes and he realizes that he's bored with you too. That's just Jack's way. He's restless. That's why we always got on so well. I helped him indulge his wild side."

Annaya raised her eyebrows in surprise at the vulgar comment and she shook her head in disbelief at how blatant the woman was being. "You have your sights on him."

"Of course I do," Hannah retorted swiftly. "Have you seen the other men available in our circles? Old, divorced, widow. He's the only bachelor in the whole of Vegas who's under forty. He's attractive, intelligent, and set to inherit everything. He'll do very well for himself and so will his wife."

"Jack's not the type to be coerced into a marriage," Annaya told her.

"He's a man, isn't he?" Hannah said slyly. "They all can be *coerced*. That's how you did it, isn't it? I can't see how else you got yourself pregnant. Is it even his?"

If Annaya had been in a different crowd, she very well may have lifted a hand to give the woman a slap for the rude comment, but instead she kept her dignity and thought of Jack's reputation and took in a little sharp breath to help her control her temper.

"Don't let Jack hear you speak like that. Alice means the world to him."

"One day he'll realize that he misses his old life. Men like Jack don't change. You'll be gone within a year."

Hannah drifted away into the crowds and Annaya was left stunned at her rudeness and boldness. She couldn't remember any time in her life that she'd ever had quite the same kind of confrontation with another woman and she was appalled at Hannah's behavior. She couldn't believe that any woman would behave like that in the desperate hope of tying down a rich man. She supposed that those who were born into it valued it much more highly than Annaya, who'd found as much joy in a night in with Natalie and a bottle of cheap Prosecco as any night dressed up in diamonds. She watched the blonde disappear and simply felt sorry for her that her priorities were so warped.

Annaya stood for a while at the edge of casino, waiting for Jack to return. She didn't know if he'd lost her in the crowds or had been pulled away again, but after ten minutes or so she decided to seek him out. She left the main body of the casino and headed out the doors towards the great sweeping staircase that lead towards the bathrooms and the upper bar. She stepped around the doorway and spotted Jack at the base of the staircase. He was not alone. With him was Hannah and she was trailing her finger up and down his chest seductively. Annaya instinctively flushed red with rage and jealously and she crept closer to listen to them speak, concealed by the staircase as she listened.

"She's pretty, Jack, I'll give you that, but she's not like us. She's mumsy, don't you think? Sure, she gave you one good night in the bedroom, but now she's tied you down she'll turn into a nag, just like every other new mom. Is that really what you want?"

Jack scowled and pushed Hannah away. "It's not a competition and even if it was, Annaya would blow you away."

Hannah bristled at that and let out a little offended

scoff. "You never used to say those kinds of things to me. Not when we were young and... *adventurous.*"

The gold-digger reached a hand out and went to reach between Jack's thighs. The billionaire's expression instantly darkened and he grabbed Hannah by the wrist, pushing her hand away from him.

"Enough. You're embarrassing yourself."

Hannah's scowl deepened. "You take the high road now and push me away like I'm some desperate whore, but you'll soon come running back when you realize that little miss perfect has turned cold and is expecting you to run errands and play the perfect daddy."

"Annie has qualities that you will never have and will never understand. She's intelligent and strong-willed and she doesn't throw her body around to get men's attention. She had self-respect and dignity and her own mind.

You can try as hard as you like with your tight dresses and wandering hands, but no matter how much your daddy earns or which circles you walk in, you will never hold a candle to her. Back away, Hannah, before you make even more of a fool of yourself."

The blonde's cheeks flared red once more and she stormed up the stairs towards the women's bathroom. Jack stayed for a moment on his step, composing himself after the confrontation and eventually turned to rejoin the gala. He came down the three steps in front of him and then came to a sudden halt when he spotted Annaya hiding behind the staircase, looking at him with her big, round eyes full of surprise and admiration.

"Annie. Are you alright? I'm sorry I've been gone so long."

"I heard what you said to that woman. Do you really think that much of me?"

"You should know what I think of you by now, Annie."

For once, Annaya didn't hesitate. She crossed the space between them in one swift step, threw both her arms around his neck and kissed him passionately. His arms tightened around her waist and pulled her closer to him and everything faded away in one perfect kiss. Annaya pulled back with her eyes sparkling and she looked up at him tenderly.

"I've never said it Jack, but I love you. I think I have for some time."

"I love you too, Annie."

"I know that there's still a lot to work out, but, if you'll still have me, I'd like to try a real relationship. No more skipping around each other. I'm ready to take a risk."

"Risks are good. Take it from an expert gambler."

Annaya looked over her shoulder at the sound of clicking and realized that a photographer had not been far behind them when they'd been kissing, but she wasn't embarrassed. She simply laughed and took hold of Jack's hand. She felt elated.

It was wonderful that finally things were falling into place. They had each other and had finally said what needed to be said. They had a beautiful daughter sleeping soundly in a glorious mansion not far away. What was left to worry them?

*

Even in the final months of her pregnancy and in the first months of her new marriage, Natalie was still looking out for Annaya and it was she who called the woman a week later with bad news that hadn't yet reached Annie's attention.

"Are you on a subscription or something?" Annie chuckled when Natalie told her that she was in the Vegas news again. "Why are you reading all those Vegas magazines?"

"Because I'm looking out for you, Annaya. You've got to be careful with the press. They'll say anything to sell stories."

"What are you saying, Nat? What have they said this time?" Annaya racked her brains to think of anything she or Jack had said at the gala that could have been spun into anything that would mar either of their reputations. She felt that they'd presented themselves well and as a team. She couldn't think of anything that she had to worry about. "Have they said anything about me?"

"Not you. Jack."

"Jack?"

"Go pick up that awful Vegas celeb mag, Annie. You'll see what I'm on about. Page three."

Annaya put Alice into her pram and left for the store immediately. Jack was out again attending to business, so she was alone when she stepped into the shop and headed for the magazine aisle. She found the magazine that Natalie had been on about and spotted the headline on the cover straight away:

Casali's Ex Reveals All - Does his new flame know his secrets?

Feeling sick, Annaya turned to page three and her eyes fell first and foremost onto the two pictures across the two-page spread. One was of her and Jack kissing by the staircase and the other was of Hannah sitting in a chair, facing the camera with a serious reveal-all expression on her face. Annaya's stomach sank.   What had the desperate woman said now? Annaya turned her attention to the first words on the page and began to read.

This week, billionaire playboy Jack Casali showed off

his latest flame, Annaya Towler, at the annual Casali Charity Gala. Shown kissing, left, the two lovebirds seemed smitten at the event, but Casali's former lover, Hannah Sawyer, left, warns the new woman in Jack's life that the billionaire has his dark side.

Annaya's mouth fell open as she began to read extracts from the article.

Sawyer described how she and the former bachelor used to spend wild nights enjoying Vegas nightlife and claims that although the playboy seems to have broken his bad habits of late, that he was always a 'bad boy'.

Hannah had the following to say about her relationship with Jack Casali: "It was wild. Every night it was a different club, a different drug, a different bedroom. Jack must have slept with half the

375

women in Vegas, but we always had a particular

spark. He was adventurous in all aspects of life, but

especially between the sheets. If he's planning on

settling down, I'm happy for him, but I'd warn the new

woman in his life to go in with her eyes open. Jack is

not a good role model and I suspect it won't be long

before he plays away."

The article went on, just more and more of the same.
The feature described Jack's wild antics over the last
ten years and had comments from more than one
woman he'd slept with. According to the article he'd
taken all kinds of drugs, slept with all kinds of
women and been involved with all kinds of scandals.

Annaya felt repulsed as she read through the tell-all
feature and felt the tears beginning to rise as she read
all about the sordid history of the man she loved.

Tearfully, she paid for the magazine and returned to the mansion.

It was a torturous day waiting for Jack to return so that she could confront him about Hannah's reveal all, but when Jack did at last arrive, he was the first to tackle the issue. He found her in the nursery with Alice on her lap and he half-ran in, falling to his knees in front of her and taking hold of her spare hand desperately. One look at her tear-stained face told him that she'd definitely seen the article.

"You'll read a lot of things about me if you do a little digging," he told her in a quiet, ashamed voice. "I'm ashamed to say that half of them are true. I've slept with my fair share of women and had a go at my fair share of vices. I've been reckless and foolish and wild. There are people in my past who'd tear me down for the cost of an article, but I swear to you, Annie, that I am a changed man and that I love you."

Annaya laid her hand on top of his and although the tears were falling again, she accepted what he had to say and nodded.

"I don't care what you've done," she told him. "I just need to know that what Hannah says isn't true. All of this, all you've done, is that what you really want? Will you grow tired of me and Alice? Is this who you are?"

"I've spent my whole life trying to feel the way you make me feel," Jack told her earnestly. "I've searched for it in sex and drugs and gambling, but that feeling I was searching for, that *elation*, that *satisfaction*, I found it with you. You're all I need, Annie. You're everything I want. There is nobody else and never will be. You could never bore me."

"How can you be sure?" Annaya said tearfully. "Hannah's right. I'm a mother now and Alice will always come first. There will be school runs and piano recitals and doctor's appointments. My party days are over. I'm never going to be like those girls again."

"You beat those girls hands down, Annie. You're incredible."

Annie looked down at him from where she sat in the nursery rocking chair. His eyes were so earnest and full of love that she believed him completely and it filled her heart with joy to think that their passion for each other had turned to love; the spark had turned into a relationship; their parenthood had turned into a life together.

Jack lifted himself slightly, just enough to reach her lips over the head of their sleeping daughter and the little family held each other close for a while, knowing that everything had changed, but it had changed for the better.

*****

Alice was eighteen months old when Brandon passed away and it was a time that was filled with great sadness and great change. After Jack had introduced Annie to the world at the gala, she'd finally felt secure enough to take a risk on him and she'd packed up her life in Bakersfield and moved to Vegas. She'd never in her life thought that she'd find herself amongst the city lights of such a wild and unpredictable place, but, strangely enough, it suited their adventurous little family.

Inheriting his father's fortune, Jack's future was sealed as a businessman and an entrepreneur. Yet, no matter how busy he found himself with work and PR meetings, Jack always found time to come back to Annaya and his little girl.

Having an endless income made the distance from Annaya's family much easier to deal with. She regularly flew out with Alice to see them and regularly flew them out to see her. Natalie loved Vegas and she also loved Jack, once she got to know them. Annie's quiet little friend was quite the gossip addict and she loved to act as Annaya's personal researcher when it came to finding out what the press had to say about them.

After that reveal-all article from Hannah, which Annaya had defiantly put behind them, the media attention eventually died down and whenever Jack and Annaya did come across their names in the papers, it was always in reference to how they were role models as parents and to how well Jack was doing following in his father's footsteps.

True to his word, he bought them a house outside of the city center, and that's where Annaya spent most of her time, giving Alice a normal upbringing in a building that was notably devoid of chandeliers, although from time to time she would let her daughter play in granddad's house, even though granddad was gone.

Annaya was proud to see her daughter growing into a sweet and patient little girl with her mother's determination and strong will and her father's spontaneity. It made her quite the handful sometimes, but Annie and Jack wouldn't have her any other way. They knew better than anybody that life was more fun with a wild streak.

Life was drastically different to what it had been, but Annaya found that the changed suited her well. She didn't work in an office anymore, but she rose to the unique challenges that came with being the partner of a rich man and showed her face at all the right corporate events and invested her time in charity work and the school boards. She was a full-time mom to Alice and it was the greatest joy she had ever known.

To make her happiness even more perfect was the fact that Jack was there with her. Annaya loved him more every single day and was so glad that they'd finally overcome all the fear and nonsense that had been keeping them apart and had confessed their love to one another. As soon as it was out in the open, and recognized for what it was, it grew and grew into something quite remarkable.

Three years later, when Alice was a toddler and Jack a respected CEO, when Natalie's child had been born and Annie was making waves in the community, the timing was finally right for a question that had been asked long ago to be asked again.

"You look beautiful," Jack told Annie when he saw her dressed in that very navy dress she'd been wearing the night they'd first met.

Annie laughed and gave him a soft kiss. "Really? Why did you want me to put this old thing on, Jack? Aren't you worried *Vogue* will come knocking on our door complaining that I'm doing a terrible job of representing women's fashion?"

"What are you on about?" Jack chuckled. "You look sensational. That's the dress you were wearing the night we met."

"I remember."

Annie smiled at him fondly and took his hand as he led her to the car. They were heading to the casino for another corporate event. Although it was chaotic inside the venue, Annaya had a soft spot for the roulette wheels and card tables, knowing that everything she had now all started here, when she took the first real gamble of her life. It seemed that Jack was keen for her to remember that time too. He held her hand as they entered through that revolving door and pointed out the poker table where he'd first seen her laying out her chips.

"That's where I first laid eyes on you. You were flirting with me."

Annaya laughed at how he told the story and gave him a playful nudge. "You were staring."

"You were wearing that dress and I couldn't take my eyes off of you. You were the most beautiful thing I'd ever seen."

"I thought you were gorgeous the moment I laid eyes on you."

Jack steered her over to the bar and helped her step up onto the stool where she'd been sitting that night.

"This is where you were sitting when I first spoke to you."

"I remember. You asked if you could steal me away

from my friends for the night."

"That's right. I knew we were in for an adventure. There was something about you that I just couldn't walk away from." The billionaire took her hand again and Annaya was confused when he lead her back out of the casino.

"Jack, where are we going?"

"It's a surprise."

Jack led her a little while down the street, past a few bars along the way. "This is where it all gets a little hazy, but I think we went in this bar and then that one."

"Yes, I remember that one!" Annaya giggled. "We played pool, didn't we?"

"Yes, I think we did. And that's the one where we did the shots."

"Oh wow! I'd forgotten about those."

Jack continued to lead her down the street and then stopped on the corner of the avenue. All around them, the neon lights were glowing and a giant screen was flashing advertisements above their heads. It was dazzling, disorientating and invigorating all at once so be surrounded by so many blinking lights and so much activity.

"The church is down the street, so I'm imagining that this is the spot where I drunkenly proposed to you that night."

Annaya giggled again and looked around bewilderedly as though something might job her memory. "I just don't remember, Jack."

"It's no matter," the billionaire said suavely. "We'll recreate the memory."

Annie turned back from looking around to see that Jack was now down on one knee and she felt her heart skip a beat. The charming billionaire was grinning up at her and holding open a ring box that contained the most dazzling diamond engagement ring that Annaya had ever seen in her life.

She gasped and her eyes grew wider when she saw that that advertisement screen above them was now playing out Jack's proposal right there and then, with the words 'Annie, will you marry me?' flashing. Annaya began to laugh in surprise and excitement and her hands flew over her mouth in astonishment.

"Annie, the first time I proposed to you, I was completely drunk and I don't remember a thing, but I'm pretty sure that even in that state, I knew that there was something special between us. A spark. The second time I proposed, I thought that the spark was enough and that the rest would come, but you were smart enough to know that a marriage needs more than chemistry to work. It needs commitment and memories and companionship and a whole load of other things to make it work and make it last.

Now, I'm proposing again. I'm sober, I'm ready to commit and I am madly in love with you. Since I've met you, Annie, I've seen our spark grow into a flame and our lives come together in so many different ways. You're a beautiful woman, an amazing partner and an incredible mother. You and Alice make me happier than I ever thought I could be. You mean the world to me and I think it's finally time to do it right. Annaya Towler, will you marry me?"

Happy laughter rose up in Annaya's throat and she threw her arms around Jack's neck elatedly, showering him with kisses. The billionaire laughed at her reaction and picked her up as he stood, spinning her under the neon Vegas lights and kissing her passionately in front of the crowd that had gathered. He slipped the ring onto her finger and Annaya trembled with excitement and joy.

Three and a half years ago, when Jack had proposed in a room full of roses, Annaya had turned him down because she was afraid that he didn't know her well enough to make a real commitment and she was afraid of settling down out of panic rather than love. Now, no doubts remained.

She loved Jack madly and over the years a deep and lasting bond had grown between them. Jack was loyal and supportive and an incredible father. He had shown her how much he loved her in public and behind closed doors. He had changed her world for the better and Annaya didn't want to live a day without him.

"Yes!" she cried out joyously. "Yes! Yes! I'll marry you!"

When Annaya walked down the aisle six months later, she remembered how her wild affair with Jack had all begun because she'd been worrying that she'd never find true love. Her best friend was getting married and Annaya was still searching for that spark that everyone else seemed to find so easily. That's when Jack walked through the door of that casino and turned her world upside down.

Looking at him waiting for her at the head of the aisle on her wedding day, Annaya felt herself being swept off her feet all over again. He was as handsome as the first time she'd ever laid eyes on him, but there was so much more between them now; not just a spark, but a history. They knew each other's secrets and had survived their first few rows and still the spark remained.

Annaya looked up at her groom and saw how much he loved her as her own heart lifted at the sight of him. Whatever happened next, she knew her future was secure. She'd finally found someone to love madly. As unexpected and wild as it had begun, her life with Jack had somehow settled into the life she'd always dreamed she'd have.

She loved Jack passionately and he loved her and

they still had all the years of their lives ahead of them

left to let that spark burn.

THE END

Fancy A FREE BWWM Romance Book??

Join the "**Romance Recommended**" Mailing list today and gain access to an exclusive **FREE** classic BWWM Romance book along with many others more to come. You will also be kept up to date on the best book deals in the future on the hottest new BWWM Romances.

* Get FREE Romance Books For Your Kindle & Other Cool giveaways

* Discover Exclusive Deals & Discounts Before Anyone Else!

* Be The FIRST To Know about Hot New Releases From Your Favorite Authors

Click The Link Below To Access This Now!

Oh Yes! Sign Me Up To Romance Recommended For FREE!

Already subscribed?

OK, Read On!

A MUST HAVE!

TALL, WHITE & ALPHA

10 BILLIONAIRE ROMANCE BOOKS BOXSET

An amazing chance to own 10 complete books for one LOW price!

This package features some of the biggest selling authors from the world of Billionaire Romance. They have collaborated to bring you this super-sized portion of love, sex and romance involving loveable heroines and Tall, White and Alpha Billionaire men.

1 The Billionaire's Designer Bride – Alexis Gold
2 The Prettiest Woman – Lena Skye
3 How To Marry A Billionaire – Susan Westwood
4 Seduced By The Italian Billionaire – CJ Howard
5 The Cowboy Billionaire's Proposal – Monica Castle
6 Seduced By The Secret Billionaire – Cherry Kay
7 Billionaire Impossible – Lacey Legend
8 Matched With The British Billionaire – Kimmy Love
9 The Billionaire's Baby Mama – Tasha Blue
10 The Billionaire's Arranged Marriage – CJ Howard

START READING THIS NOW AT THE BELOW LINKS

Amazon.com > http://www.amazon.com/Tall-White-Alpha-Billionaire-Collection-ebook/dp/B0115KNSMA/

Amazon.co.uk > http://www.amazon.co.uk/Tall-White-Alpha-Billionaire-Collection-ebook/dp/B0115KNSMA/

Amazon.ca > http://www.amazon.ca/Tall-White-Alpha-Billionaire-Collection-ebook/dp/B0115KNSMA/

Amazon.com.au > http://www.amazon.com.au/Tall-White-Alpha-Billionaire-Collection-ebook/dp/B0115KNSMA/

Printed in Great Britain
by Amazon